The

Sentient

Advantage

Chris Pugmire

Llumina Press

Requests for permission to make copies of any part of this work should be mailed to Permissions Department, Llumina Press, PO Box 772246, Coral Springs, FL 33077-2246

ISBN: 978-1-62550-378-7

Printed in the United States of America by Llumina Press

Authors Note

When I first wrote this book I wanted to enjoy reading it as if someone else had written it. So, I came up with the cunning plan of waiting 10 years without thinking about it and then re-reading it. Surprisingly, my plan mostly worked; and even more surprisingly, I found that I really quite liked it and decided to get it published.

If you liked this book, then drop me an email to chris@netwin.co.nz; then please go to your local bookstore and buy another copy (ask them to order it if they don't have it in stock, and politely suggest they should stock it). And then, send it to a friend as an unexpected gift.

If you didn't like this book, then go and buy a second copy anyway. Send it to someone you don't like.

Every year 100,000 new books are published and only a small fraction of those make it to your local book shop. With all the competition you would expect there to be an endless supply of really excellent books but unfortunately it's easier to sell another book from a famous author. So when you find a book you like, please take the time to promote it, if everyone does this then we will all get to read more good books, also it's a very cheap way to give someone several hours of pleasure without **anyone** getting arrested.

CHAPTER ONE

Jaros opened his eyes; he was falling, his hands grabbed wildly but nothing was in reach. Adrenaline surged through him as he realized death would be instant, but after several seconds elapsed it became clear he was not dead, but incredibly, was still falling. Twisting to look down his eyes eventually focused on lights far below.

"Oh great," he said to himself. "I won't be dead for another minute or two at least."

He started looking for a rip cord, but couldn't find anything that was obviously right. He was wearing a suit of some kind, complete with helmet and visor, almost like a space suit. There was no cord.

He wondered briefly how he had gotten himself into this rather awkward situation. He cast his mind back, and hit nothing. A blank. A chill ran down his spine. He was about to die and he didn't know why.

The lights were getting brighter. He didn't have long now. His mind was racing. Surely there was something that he should do before the end, some great insight. He wished briefly that he had a pen and paper handy incase he did think of something profound. It would be such a pity to die without being able to write it down first.

Then a thought struck him. "Maybe I'm dreaming." He clung to it as it seemed to offer the best chance of survival. Reaching down with his fingers he tried to pinch his leg. But the suit he was wearing prevented him. "I bet that's just the bed clothes, and my arm is outside the bed." He waved his arm around madly trying to get it inside his invisible bed, but to no avail.

Suddenly he was hit by something. His whole body jerked like a rag doll, swinging madly for a second before the world stabilized again. Looking up he saw the parachute dimly in the dark sky above, and experienced an almost overwhelming sense of relief and joy.

"Well that was a good idea." He said to no one in particular. He was still grinning stupidly to himself feeling smug for no real reason at all when he remembered that the ground was still coming towards him at what could be a fairly painful speed. Since it was dark the chances of a soft controlled landing seemed slim, particularly since he had no memory of being trained in how to land a parachute.

Looking down again he tried to make out what was below. He could see patches of lights, lines and squares, and darker areas with no real form, possibly fields. He felt it would probably be wise to try to land in one of the darker area's. He reached up to try and grab some kind of steering cords, but found nothing. Then, with some alarm, he noticed a metallic device some 6 feet above him at the point where the parachute lines joined.

"What on earth is that?" he wondered out loud. The thing was making buzzing sounds and he could see the cords moving in and out of it. At the same time he would feel himself swaying left and right.

The dark patches he'd been hoping to steer for were now expanding rapidly and he could see he was heading for one of them. But now his eyes picked out something else. Little lines of white appearing, and then disappearing. He was mesmerized for what seemed like minutes as the patterns moved, vanished and reformed. Then the cold reality suddenly struck him. Waves!

Feeling sick this time as more adrenaline fed his already overly active imagination he considered the chances of surviving once he hit the water. Assuming he could swim at all, and even that basic fact escaped him.

For the last few seconds he just stared at the water rushing towards him. "Oh crap." he thought. This is going to be painful, cold and fatal. A most unhappy combination.

Suddenly he hit the water. The blackness swallowed him instantly. Cold and terrified he held his breath, waiting for the end. He was not prepared to open his mouth and let the water choke him until he had to. He held his breath as the painful cold started to seep through whatever he was wearing. Then his feet hit something. He kicked off it madly without even thinking, his lungs bursting, he must be meters under the water, but maybe he could make it to the surface.

His feet touched bottom again. His suit must be made of lead. Finally he couldn't wait any longer and he sucked in madly hoping to die in seconds and avoid prolonging the torture any longer. With some surprise he found he was still breathing air.

"You really should get moving," said a voice in his ear.

Jaros practically screamed in surprise, "Who said that?"

"The beach is about 200 meters to your right. It should only take a few minutes if you start now. There isn't much air in this suit so it would probably be a good idea to get a move along."

"Hello, can you hear me. What's going on? Are you receiving?"

Jaros waited for a response, but nothing, just silence now. He considered whether he should simply sit and wait for the voice to say something else, but the cold and the fear of death or disorientation prevented him. He turned carefully to his right, moving slowly in the water. He started partly walking, partly swimming and partly jumping in the direction he thought the voice had meant. After a few steps he felt he could discern a slight upward slope which gave him some feeling of confidence.

Finally he felt his helmet break the surface. He pushed forward excitedly trying to get further out until he felt the water level suddenly dropping around him. His pleasure was replaced with undiluted fear as the sound of something like a freight train thundered behind him. Turning, now waist-deep in water he just saw the 8 foot tall wave for a fraction of a second before he was hit and found himself tumbling in the water.

When the churning stopped he found ground underneath and stood. Then started running as fast as he could. He didn't fancy being hit again. With great relief he stumbled out of the surf onto wet sand and made himself keep moving until he was standing well clear of the high water mark.

Fumbling with his suit he wanted to breathe real air and although he didn't know what he was doing his fingers seemed to know how to release the helmet. A cold wind blew over his face as the helmet fell to the ground. He undid the fastenings and stripped his wet outer garment off. Shivering he headed inland towards the lights in the distance.

After an hour or so he came to a small road. It was empty but he decided to follow it anyway. He trudged along unhappily his arms wrapped around himself trying to keep some warmth in.

Startled he turned to find a car had pulled up beside him, and opened it's passenger door. The word "TAXI" appeared in glowing letters on it's roof. "Darned electric motors!" he thought. "Can't hear them coming."

"Excuse me Sir, would you be Jaros?"

Jaros stared at the car for a second, before quickly stepping in simply to get warm, "Yes," he said.

"Sorry I'm late picking you up, I do hope you haven't been waiting long, I've been going up and down this road for some time now trying to find you, I'm really not programmed to cope with a pickup point like this you know, I do wish you'd told me a specific location, I really would recommend it in future."

Jaros sat in the back of the taxi still shivering, and not really listening to the computerized tin can. "Can you turn up the heating and close the door?"

"Yes certainly Sir. And the clothes you requested are in that bag."

Jaros stared at the speaker grill, then opened the bag and stared at the clothing and the towel, which he quickly made use of before changing.

After doing this his mind eventually caught up with something it had been processing. "Who did you say ordered you?"

"Why, you did, Sir. Two and a half hours ago."

Jaros was extremely cross. He had been starting to fantasize about some kind of revenge but now it seemed any such pleasure would be self inflicted and possibly not entirely satisfying.

"Did I happen to mention where I wanted to go?" he asked hopefully.

"Yes of course Sir," The cab's AI was not overly intelligent so failed to recognize the strangeness of the question.

"Oh good. Off we go then."

"Very well, Sir," responded the taxi speeding off down the road.

Jaros sat in the back warming up rapidly and feeling quite good about being alive and relatively safe. However he was also exhausted, and some time later he drifted off to sleep.

A buzzing sound intruded on his dream. The girl vanished as he opened his eyes. An insistent buzzing sound was almost echoing inside the small cab.

"Please excuse me Sir, I hate to use such harsh sounds but I have a call for you and I thought it might be urgent. Shall I activate the vid screen?"

"Yes. Go ahead."

Jaros jumped hitting his head on the roof when the picture appeared. Looking back at him was the girl from his dream; her intent blue eyes made his heart race and she flashed him a dazzling smile.

"Hi, I'm returning your call, I do hope it's not a bad time," she said.

Jaros stared blankly for a moment before regaining his wits. "Thanks."

"So?" she asked.

"Oh, I called you, did I?" By this time Jaros wasn't even slightly surprised at the response.

"Yes. Was it about the room?" she asked.

Jaros hesitated. Room? Room? What room? He was unsure of how to respond.

She prompted him, "You must have seen my advert; you know, the room with a ghost. Are you interested? Would you like to see it?"

"I believe I would," Jaros smiled to himself. Well, he was almost certain he did, or someone wanted him to.

"How does eleven o'clock sound? The address is 24 Nordale Ave. Sunny View. It is the blue house on the left after the big yellow transit station. Do you know the area?"

"Yes... Well, no ... But the car will find it."

"Yes, it shouldn't have any trouble! See you soon then."

The screen went blank. Jaros noticed it was now daylight outside. He turned to the cab's console, "Let me guess. We are already heading to Sunny View?"

"Yes, Sir, of course. We will be there shortly."

Jaros had a nagging feeling that he didn't have control over his life. He wondered briefly if this was his normal state.

Kayla turned away as the vidcom went blank. She hoped her emotions hadn't shown. She had long since given up being surprised at odd things. After all, when you have a ghost, you get used to the unusual. But was it normal to feel your heart race and face flush at the first sight of a complete stranger? Sure, he was nice to look at, maybe even handsome... She had to shake herself to start thinking again; her mind had stalled while calling up his image. What was wrong with her?

She found herself thinking of her brother Mark. He hadn't stopped by for a few days. His duties at the space academy left him with little spare time. It was his fault she had to rent out the room. For the first week or two after he left she had been okay, but then she started getting strange feelings late at night as if someone was watching her. The house was too big to be alone in at night.

That was it! The guy on the vidcom looked a little like her brother Mark. Kayla felt better having found a rational explanation for her reaction.

She started tidying up the house in a slightly nervous fashion and tried not to analyze any further. Alfred interrupted long before she was satisfied.

"Miss, there appears to be a young man approaching the house."

"Thanks Alfred. I'll answer it."

"I'm afraid I've already let him in Miss; you'll find him waiting in the lounge."

Kayla was stunned. Alfred had always been a rather unusual house comp, but letting complete strangers into the house was a new twist.

"Hi," said Kayla as she entered the lounge. "Alfred seems to have taken a liking to you. He won't let most of my friends in unless I stand with my foot jamming the door open."

Jaros grinned. "How strange. I'm Jaros. I rang earlier." His voice was low, with a slight husky quality to it.

The same strange feeling hit her again as Jaros turned from the old fire place and smiled back at her. Only the feeling was stronger now, much stronger, and she still didn't know what to make of it. He was tall and athletic with sandy hair and the most incredible green eyes. She'd seen good looking guys before but she detected an unusual quality about him, "Do you want to have a look round?" she said at last pulling her gaze away from his.

"Yes. That would be good."

Kayla led him back through the hall into the first bedroom. She was feeling extremely self-conscious. "This is my room," she said, moving past it quickly so that he didn't see too much of the mess. "And this is the room that's available. I can move the bed and stuff if you have your own furniture."

"No, it's fine as it is. I haven't got much, anyway."

Kayla led him into the kitchen, "The place is a bit old, as you can see, but it's not bad for its age. My parents left it to Mark and me; he's my younger brother."

"What do you do for a living?" asked Jaros.

"I'm a programmer, mostly."

"I thought comps did that sort of stuff these days."

"Cripes no! Not on anything important anyway. There's no telling what those half-witted things would come up with. They don't understand humans very well, and the tricky bit of writing a program is figuring out what the human client actually wants the program to do."

Jaros nodded, "I think I've seen enough. When can you let me know if I can have the room?"

Kayla grinned; she had almost given up hope that anyone would answer the advert, let alone someone she actually liked. After three weeks of adverts with not a single response. She had been starting to suspect Alfred was blocking the calls. But every time she suggested giving up he had insisted she keep trying. Anyway, now her problems were over. "No one else has rung so the room is yours. When do you want to move in?"

Jaros considered his other options. "Umm, right now would be good."

"Okay, great. I'll be in all day; and I think Alfred will probably let you in whether I tell him to or not."

A voice burst from the walls, "I would not dream of taking such liberties, Miss."

Kayla smiled dubiously, "Of course you wouldn't. I was just joking. But now that I'm asking, you will let Jaros come and go freely?"

"But of course, Miss."

Jaros cut in, "Your advert mentioned a ghost didn't it?"

"Oh, don't worry. He's a friendly ghost," said Kayla with a mischievous grin.

That appeared to be all she was going to say for the moment and Jaros didn't care to press the point. He was sure he would find out more, probably sooner than he liked, and he had his own mysteries to think about.

CHAPTER TWO

Jaros awoke early. The sun was blazing through a gap between the curtains. He sat up and began to think. There had to be a reason for his memory loss. He tried to remember all he could about memory problems but quickly realized that in his current state, there was a problem with that method of research.

"Alfred?" he asked.

"Yes, sir?"

"What do you know about memory loss?"

"A great deal, sir, as indeed I know a great deal about many things. Could sir narrow down the field with a more specific request?"

"Summarize the means by which someone might lose their memory."

"You are referring to human memories, are you not?"

"Yes," replied Jaros, wondering at the way Alfred managed to impart an ever so slightly inferior tone to the word human.

"A friend, perhaps?" asked Alfred.

Jaros started to feel as if he was losing control of the conversation. "If you don't know the answer, just say so!"

"Of course I can answer the question, sir. I was merely trying to establish the nature of the information you required so as to avoid wasting your time with anything that wasn't entirely relevant."

"Well, get on with it, then," said Jaros, while he dressed and made a mental note to buy some more clothes. He wondered briefly with a slight grin if perhaps he should write it down. Maybe his memory was erased regularly.

Alfred continued, "There are two general mechanisms that can be involved. The most common is physical. For example, a blow to the head. The second mechanism, and possibly more dubious is psychological trauma. Humans appear to have the ability to spontaneously forget certain events. This second method is particularly common in relation to events of a distressing nature."

"Okay, thanks," said Jaros as he wandered out toward the kitchen with thoughts of muffins, bacon and a really good cup of tea.

In the kitchen he found Kayla standing at the sink.

"Morning" he said.

Kayla turned, looking a little startled and then smiled warmly. "Did you have a good night?"

"Yes thanks. Great bed."

"There's some bran-mix in the cupboard and wholemeal bread over there," Kayla pointed at the bread bin. "Milk is in the fridge."

"You're not a bacon and eggs breakfast person, then?" asked Jaros hopefully.

Kayla laughed.

Jaros soon found himself eating a very unpleasant bowl of high-bran, low fat, high-carbohydrate, low-sugar unprocessed cardboard. "It's delicious," he lied. "I wish I'd discovered this stuff years ago."

"Sorry, I guess I shouldn't boss you around like I do with my brother. If you want to eat something else, don't let me stop you.

Jaros smiled, "No need to apologize. I really rather liked being treated like that, I think it reminds me of home; and I need all the reminding I can get at the moment."

"In that case," said Kayla, grinning mischievously and switching to her 'in charge' voice, "Stop playing with your spoon and start eating. It may taste like wood filings, but it will make you live longer."

Jaros grinned back at her and munched happily on the tasteless cereal, contemplating his situation and trying to remember why being ordered to eat was so pleasant. Strangely it reminded him of home, even though he had absolutely no memory of what home was. On the other hand, it was nice just being around Kayla so maybe he was just imagining a home he would like to exist.

Jaros spent most of the day trying to track down something of his past, but all his leads turned up blank. His credit account had been opened anonymously two days earlier. It was the only item he'd found in his clothing, a credit card with the name "Jaros Smith" on it.

He tried the phone book, but found over two hundred Jaros Smiths just in the local district and he suspected he wasn't a local even assuming his name really was Jaros Smith, which didn't seem entirely likely.

Going to the police was a possibility, but didn't seem wise just yet. There might be a very good reason for him not to let every Tom, Dick and Constable Harry in on a secret that apparently his other self didn't want him to know.

He was tempted to ask Kayla her opinion. He needed to talk to someone about it, but he didn't know her well enough yet. Besides she probably thought he was strange enough already. She might just call for the men in white coats herself if she knew exactly how mixed up his head was.

Kayla came in exhausted from work. She tried not to look into the lounge as she walked past, but her gaze lingered on him longer than necessary as she made her way past the door into the kitchen.

"Alfred, can you make me something to eat? I can't be bothered at the moment."

"Certainly miss. Would you like something in particular or should I surprise you?"

"Surprise me."

Within seconds a tray and a large mug emerged from the wall, the contents of the tray were not entirely familiar, or even vaguely recognizable, but Kayla was used to Alfred's cooking and didn't really care. "Thanks, it looks delicious."

Kayla picked up the tray. Normally she would eat in the lounge, but Jaros was in there and she didn't like to intrude. The longer she stood thinking about joining Jaros, the more nervous she got. Finally, she took a long swallow from the mug, and clasping the tray firmly, walked purposefully into the lounge.

Jaros grinned up at her as she entered. She had a strange feeling that he'd been watching the door, waiting for her to come in.

Kayla sat down and ate in silence, pretending to be totally absorbed in the vid and her meal.

"Why is the light swinging?" asked Jaros, concerned.

Kayla didn't even glance upwards. "It's the ghost; he does things like that just to let me know he's around."

Jaros continued to stare at the light. It slowly swung less and less until eventually it was completely still. "How long has the house been haunted?" he asked.

Kayla suspected Jaros was making fun of her, but she didn't really mind. The fun of watching people when they realized they were wrong always made up for it. "I don't really know. Ever since I can remember odd things have been happening."

"What sort of odd things?"

"The usual haunted house stuff. Strange sounds at night, objects vanishing and then turning up later in places they couldn't possibly be. One time I found a photo of Mark on the roof of the house. All sorts of things."

"But you haven't actually seen any headless ghosts strolling around the house?"

Kayla leaned forward conspiratorially and whispered, "Well, I've had some strange dreams lately, with large hairy creatures chasing me down the hall, but no actual headless ghosts. Sorry."

Suddenly Jaros yelped and jerked forward, knocking the coffee table over in the process.

"Something touched me," he exclaimed, looking over his shoulder.

Kayla couldn't stop herself from laughing. "I expect it was probably the ghost."

Later that night Jaros was still feeling foolish as he climbed into bed. He hated having made such an idiot of himself in front of her. On the other hand, she had obviously found it tremendously amusing; and anything that made Kayla laugh was ok, even if he had to look a little silly in the process.

"Fade lights out please, Alfred."

"I could leave them on just a little if that would make you feel better, sir?"

Alfred's tone managed to convey just a hint of enjoyment. "No thank you, just fade them out normally."

Jaros drifted off to sleep, wondering if his dreams would bring answers to any of the mysteries that surrounded him.

Jaros woke with a start; it must be after midnight, had he heard something? Why was he awake? For a few moments he lay completely still, trying not to breathe so he could listen for the smallest sound...no nothing, it must have been a dream. He rolled over and closed his eyes intent on getting back to sleep.

Thump!

What was that? Something in the hall? Something large! He froze, listening intently, ready to leap out of bed and into action at any second. Why was he so jumpy? It was probably just Kayla going to the bathroom, but then he remembered the bathroom wasn't actually in that direction from Kayla's room.

He took a deep breath and quietly climbed out of bed. Shivering slightly in the chill night he crept slowly over to his bedroom door, feeling his way with his hands in the dark. Turning the handle as slowly as possible he inched it open just enough to look down the hall. Seeing nothing, he turned to go back to bed but found his feet were stuck to the floor. His heart raced as he pulled at the ground and heard the thumps of something large charging down the hall behind him. Still struggling Jaros peered over his shoulder to see his attacker. Just as he turned a blood curdling scream broke the blackness of the night; he bolted upright in bed. Beads of sweat dripped down his face as he panted for breath.

He hadn't screamed. He heard it again, someone was screaming and it wasn't him. It must be Kayla! He flew out through the doorway, bounced off the wall, and raced down the hall into Kayla's room.

The lights came on before he got there. The bed was a crumpled mess. Kayla was sitting with her knees pulled up close, and the bedclothes pulled up like a shield. Jaros spun around scanning the room but saw nothing unusual.

"What happened?" he asked, stepping closer.

Kayla looked at him blankly and then suddenly her eyes focused, "Jaros... I think I was having a nightmare."

"Are you all right?"

"I think so. Sorry for waking you. I feel so silly. You must think I'm some kind of half-baked fruitcake."

"No, not really, more of a bran muffin actually. You are what you eat." He gave her a lopsided grin.

Kayla laughed weakly. "Seriously, that is the worst pun I've heard since Mark left."

Jaros smiled, "I do my best. Anyway, it's no trouble. I'll be asleep again in no time. I guess I'll see you in the morning then?"

"Wait. Would you mind talking with me for a few minutes? I don't want to go back to sleep right away."

"Sure." He said while sitting down on the edge of the bed. "Have you had these nightmares before?"

"No, not until a few days ago. Only after Mark left for the final part of patrol training."

"What are the dreams about?"

Kayla had been sitting with her knees pulled up to her chin, but now she lay back down, moving slightly closer to Jaros in the process. "I'm not sure exactly.

Something is searching for me. I can't see it. I'm hiding and I can hear it getting closer. Then I see its shadow and I start to run. I can hear it catching up to me, but I'm too scared to look back. Then suddenly I feel something grabbing at my shoulder. I scream and that's when I usually wake up."

"How do you feel when you wake up?"

"That's the worst part. I feel like 'it' is hiding in the room, or just outside in the corridor. I usually can't sleep again."

"Do you think it has anything to do with your ghost?"

Kayla sounded surprised, "No, my ghost is friendly, it looks after me. It's never frightened me."

Jaros put on his best German accent, "Vell, I suspect your problems all stem from early childhood. Can you zink of any early experiences vich may have zubconsciously envected your mind?"

Kayla giggled, then thought for a few seconds, "There was the time I got expelled from school. Do you think that might be relevant doctor?"

"Vell, it kud be, tell me vot happened?"

"Well I kind of blew up the chemistry labs."

Jaros was too surprized to continue his accent, "How did you manage that?" he asked.

Kayla flushed, "I didn't, well at least I don't think I did. I don't remember exactly what happened, but I don't think I left the gas on like they claimed. I'm almost certain it wasn't me. The school did get a new lab out of it and no one was hurt. Well no one I liked or not seriously anyway."

Jaros grinned, "No one you seriously liked got hurt, or no one you didn't like was seriously hurt?"

Kayla thought back through what she'd said for a moment, "Both." she said at last smiling. "But do you mind if we talk about you instead? Tell me something about your sordid past."

Jaros thought for a second. "I can't."

"Come on, I've just told you some things. It's only fair," she persisted.

"No, it's not that I don't want to. I just can't." Jaros paused again, wondering if he should tell her. "The night before last I woke up in an awkward situation which doesn't really bear remembering, and before I knew it I found myself talking to you on the vid about this room. Then I came over. There, now you know my entire life story."

"I don't believe you."

"It's true. I could add a bit more but it wouldn't make it easier to believe"

"Are you serious?"

"Yes, my memories begin yesterday. I spent most of today trying to find some clues. I even checked the credit card company records, but the address they had for me turned out to belong to a new office block which hasn't been completed yet."

Kayla thought for a few seconds, "Have you contacted the police? You may have been reported as a missing person by now."

"I don't think I should yet. I have this funny feeling that I'm not supposed to know who I am, if that makes any sense at all." He gave her a speculative look. "You must think I'm a complete nutcase."

Kayla laughed, "Me, the arsonist with nightmares and a ghost?"

Jaros stood, "You sound like you've cheered up a bit. I'd better be going to bed - unless you want me to stay until you fall asleep again?"

"Would you mind?" Her gaze held his.

"Sure, if you want." He'd only been joking. But he could tell from her voice that Kayla was not. She must be really rattled.

Kayla looked towards the comp sensor, "Light fade please Alfred."

Jaros sat back down on the bed and tried to look relaxed, expecting to have to wait quite some time. He wasn't unhappy about it. He watched Kayla as her breathing became slower. Her long hair draped around her face.

Once he was sure she was soundly asleep, he carefully stood up and tiptoed out of the room.

The next morning Kayla awoke and dreamily reached out for Jaros, but he was gone.

Drat, she thought, I could hardly be more obvious than that; he hadn't taken a single hint. She'd done everything short of dragging him under the covers by force.

Jaros was lying awake in his bed, avoiding the painful reality of getting dressed, when suddenly a voice broke into his semi-conscious state.

"Excuse me, sir?"

"Yes, Alfred."

"How did you know Kayla was in trouble last night?"

"Her scream woke me."

"Are you sure?"

"Yes, of course I am. I could hardly stay asleep with someone screaming just across the hall."

"That is most interesting."

"Why?"

"Because you were already up and running down the hall when she screamed."

"That's not the way I remember it. Are you certain?"

"Yes. I have it on tape from my internal house cameras, if you'd like to see for yourself."

"No that's okay. I'll take your word for it." Jaros pondered this bit of information for a moment and then said, "Oh!"

"My thoughts exactly, sir."

Kayla took her time in the bathroom. It was Saturday morning, so there was no rush, and she wanted to look nice. Pausing in front of the mirror, she considered a new hairstyle, but decided to stick with the safe option instead.

She came out wearing her jeans and a T-shirt. The front door was open and she could see Jaros drinking his coffee, sitting on the edge of the veranda, dangling his feet over the lawn.

"What's this stuff on the ground?" he asked.

Kayla went out onto the porch to see what he was talking about. It was a clear day and already pleasantly warm. She glanced at the ground for a few seconds, "What stuff are you talking about?"

"The green stuff. Made of lots of long thin bits, each one neatly folded and curving to a point."

"Are you serious?"

"Yes, I haven't seen it before, it looks terribly intricate. Does it cost much to lay?"

Kayla remembered the strange things he'd been saying last night. "You don't lay grass; you plant it." She explained patiently watching to see how he would react.

Jaros looked confused for a second, then quickly pulled his feet up off the ground. "You mean it's alive?"

"Of course it is. You can't have forgotten about grass," she said.

"Well, I seem to have, but in this case I wonder if I ever knew," he eyed the grass with some suspicion. "I'm pretty sure this is something I'd remember."

Kayla watched him, trying to read his expression. As far as she could tell he wasn't pulling her leg. "What else do you notice as different?" she asked.

"The roads, they're too wide — much too wide — and the teller comps, their card slot is in completely the wrong place. And there is something funny about the place you wave your hand to open a door, I think it's too low."

"Alfred, do you know of any places where the roads are thin, the teller machines are different, the doors have higher sensors, and there isn't any grass?"

"I expect there may be somewhere Miss. However, I cannot find it in any database that I have access to at the moment. Possibly I am failing to construct the search parameters correctly to find it."

It was most unlike Alfred to admit to a personal failure; and Kayla didn't know what that could mean. Anyway, it was too early in the morning to think about it, so she went back inside to get some breakfast.

Jaros watched her walk back in and then turned back to examine the grass in greater detail. He was interrupted when Kayla came back out eating a large jam muffin and drinking a glass of milk.

Eventually, Kayla noticed him staring at her. "Something wrong?" she asked.

"And you didn't think to mention that you had muffins in the cupboard until after I suffered through yet another bowl of the crud you call breakfast?"

"Oh, sorry."

"No you aren't."

"No, not really," she admitted. "Seeing that expression on your face is really well worth it."

Jaros was trying to think of a suitably cutting reply when Alfred interrupted.

"Excuse me, Miss. Your brother has arrived."

"Tell him we're out here," Kayla said.

"Very good, Miss."

Jaros looked up to see a tall young man coming out onto the veranda. His sandy hair was trimmed short and he wore biking shorts that accentuated his lanky build. There was something odd about his appearance, but Jaros couldn't quite spot what it was,

"Hi, sis."

"Hi, Mark. Mark, this is Jaros. Jaros, this is Mark."

Kayla watched as they stared at each other. They almost looked like brothers, except that real siblings look different but similar, whereas they looked similar but different.

"Kayla tells me you are in the space patrol. That seems like an odd career move."

"Not really. It gives me pilot training in everything from airplanes to the interstellar transport ships, not to mention the academic degrees that go along with it, and all I have to do is give three years bonded service at the end of training."

"So you didn't join just for excitement and adventure?"

Mark grinned. "No, of course not."

"Fibber," Kayla poked him on her way back into the kitchen to find something else to eat. "You've done nothing but talk about flying one of those two-man patrol ships since you were ten years old."

"We've just started training on those. That's why I haven't been round for a couple of weeks; it's been flat out. Hey, sis. Didn't you do some work on one of the comp systems in them a few months ago?"

"Yes, but those military idiots took me off the problem when I complained that the whole system was designed wrong. The spatial addressing was far more complex than it should have been for a craft with that range. I guess maybe they over-engineered it. But it seemed a bit strange to me. Typical military mind set; first over design the requirements, and then realize all the hardware would need to be upgraded to cope with the new software - all completely pointless! Unless there is some new anti matter drive on the way. You haven't heard of any advances, have you?"

"No, I don't see how they can improve it. The limiting factor isn't the drive; it's the crew inside, who would get squashed if they put out any more oomph than they do now."

"Why did you want to know?" Kayla asked.

"Oh, it may be nothing, but the training doesn't make sense. It feels a bit like they are teaching us to do something extra; but if we ask about the things that don't make sense, we just get yelled at."

"You think that's odd? Jaros here doesn't have a past. He popped into existence yesterday morning and doesn't know what grass is. Apart from that, he seems fairly normal."

"Really?"

Jaros was a little taken back at having his secret revealed so matter-of-factly, but he didn't like to be out-cooled. "Yep, not a single clear memory more than twenty-four hours old."

Mark smiled, "I'm glad you adopted me, sis. You seem to attract mysteries like a magnet; it makes life real interesting. Like the mystery of how Alfred manages to follow us around from place to place."

"Huh?" inquired Jaros.

Mark explained, "You see. Alfred was the comp at the orphanage we lived in, and then when we were adopted he turned up at our parents' place. He'd never admit it, but we could tell it was him; normal comps don't behave that way."

Jaros was still confused about the last thing Mark had said. "If you're brother and sister, then how did Kayla adopt you?"

"Kayla has always been there for me. When Kayla got adopted. I did as well. I suspect she told our parents that we came together or not at all, but she denies any such thing."

"Huh!" exclaimed Kayla. "I've been trying to lose you in a forest somewhere ever since, but you keep turning up like a bad penny."

"Don't tell lies, sis. I'm bigger than you are now."

"You've been bigger than me for about ten years now but were always too dumb to realize it. Anyway, I can still out-wrestle you. I got a lot of practice in the orphanage before the right foster parents turned up!" She gave Mark a playful hug, which he struggled out of awkwardly.

Jaros stood up. "I've got some more research to do on my little mysteries, and so I'd better be going. Nice to meet you, Mark. I'll see you later, Kayla."

"Don't be too late back tonight. I'll help you do some searches on the net if you like."

"Great. Bye."

Kayla watched him leave and then turned to Mark and dragged him by the hand down into the garden. "Come with me, I want to have a chat."

"This sounds ominous; I didn't think I'd done anything lately that would require a lecture, or anything you'd know about, anyway."

"Mark, I have a problem."

"Don't tell me you've blown up your dishwasher again, I told you I'm not going to fix it anymore!"

"No, this is serious. There's something strange about Jaros."

"What do you mean?" Asked Mark suddenly concerned.

"Well, it's not really Jaros that's strange. It's what happens to me when I'm near him." Kayla hesitated nervously.

"Yes?" prompted Mark.

"He makes me feel odd, a bit like an adrenaline rush, except it's continuous... I start talking quickly and making bad jokes and saying things I wouldn't normally say."

Mark grinned, "... And your problem is?"

Kayla nibbled at her hair. "I don't know, it's just..." She trailed off when she looked up. "Why are you grinning at me like that? Stop it!"

"Oh, come on, I may have only met him five minutes ago but even in that time I can see the way you two couldn't stop looking at each other. And after what you just said, it would take a blind idiot not to see what the problem is. I know you haven't dated many guys, but don't tell me you don't know what being in love feels like!"

Kayla stared at her brother for a few seconds. "No! He's just a friend."

"Are you really saying you don't fancy him at all?"

"No," said Kayla, more to herself than to Mark. "Maybe I find him attractive but that wouldn't explain this? It's been like this since the first time I saw him. I don't know him well enough to be in love and anyway it doesn't feel good, it feels terrible!"

By this time Mark had realized how upset she was. "There's a reason they call it 'lovesick,' you know."

"But what if I don't want to be in love?"

"I could quote Shakespeare, but I think paraphrasing will make it clearer. 'You don't choose with whom you fall in love, it just happens.' Life would be a lot simpler if romance were a rational business."

Kayla gazed at the ground, lost in her own thoughts. She couldn't be in love without actually deciding to be in love; it was just silly. Anyway, that was not how it was supposed to work, so she wouldn't accept it. Stubborn was something she was very good at. Finally she remembered that Mark was still looking at her with his best worried expression. "I bet you couldn't really quote Shakespeare!"

"'The lady doth protest too much, methinks.' Hamlet Act III, Scene II, or perhaps you would prefer something even more appropriate, 'The course of true love never did run smooth'".

"Ok, so you can. Let me guess; you were trying to impress some girl and memorized a bunch of romantic quotes so you could appear to be sensitive and arty. Right?"

Mark grinned, "Sounds like a good plan. Do you think it would work?"

"No."

CHAPTER THREE

*I*n the early hours next morning Jaros found himself awake suddenly without knowing why. At first he thought Kayla was having another nightmare, but there was no screaming. There was only a scratching sound. He tried not to breathe for a few seconds so he could hear it again, yes!

"Alfred," he whispered.

"Yes, sir?"

"Do you have any sensors around the sides of the house?"

"Regrettably not, sir."

"So if someone was out there trying to get in, you wouldn't know, would you?"

"Are you referring to that scraping sound, sir?"

"Yes."

"It only started a few moments ago. I was considering waking you."

"I've got a bad feeling about it. Can you pick up anything on the external cameras?

"I am attempting to use our neighbour's cameras to get a clear view of the side of the house, but they are not designed to work at such a long range. Under these lighting conditions I can't get a clear picture, but I suggest you and Kayla prepare for the worst. I have just woken her and appraised her of the situation. You should dress as quietly as possible."

Jaros threw on his clothes and sneakers while he wondered what the worst could be. After grabbing his credit card, he quickly looked around the room and through the closet until he spotted Mark's tennis racquet. He picked it up, weighing it in his hand, before tiptoeing out of his room.

Jaros met Kayla in the hall. He motioned her to keep quiet and follow him. Together they crept down to the kitchen.

Alfred's voice was barely audible from the speakers in the kitchen, "I've succeeded in getting a clear picture of them. There are at least three large bipedal creatures trying to break into the house. They don't appear to be human. I suggest you close the door leading from the kitchen into the rest of the house, and pile as much stuff up against it as possible. I will attempt to trap them in the front part of the house."

Jaros and Kayla dragged the fridge across the door.

"Okay," said Alfred. "Wait by the back door. I'm opening the front to let them in. As soon as they enter, I'll shut that door and open the back door so that you two can make a run for the car."

They waited in silence, holding their breath for what seemed like ages. Suddenly they heard the sounds of heavy feet stomping up through the hall. Alfred slid the back door open and Jaros jumped out. He was almost round the corner of the house before he realized that Kayla wasn't behind him. He turned and raced back, only to find her coming out. She was stuffing an object into her pocket.

They jumped in the car and switched it on. "Go! As fast as possible!" away from here." Jaros urged the car.

Kayla interrupted, "Stop at the top of the hill, but keep the engine running."

"Why?" asked Jaros.

"You'll see."

The car pulled to a halt at the top of the hill as instructed. Kayla turned to watch the house.

"What are we watching for?" asked Jaros.

"Ssh. Any second now."

They waited and watched. From this distance the house appeared quiet and peaceful. Suddenly, the entire roof jumped several feet in the air; and the house was encased in a ball of flame.

"I had a relapse," explained Kayla.

"But why?"

"Just before the door opened, Alfred displayed the picture of them on the vid screen. You didn't notice, but just the sight of them sent shivers down me. I was certain they were the same as the creature in my dream, the ones I never see. Yes I know that doesn't make sense but somehow I recognized them."

"So you turned the gas on?"

"Basically, yes."

"But what about Alfred?"

Kayla pulled out a large object from her pocket, "I think this is him. I watched a serviceman installing it shortly after we first moved into the house, and the next day the house comp had turned into Alfred."

Jaros suddenly stared back at the house.

Kayla followed his gaze to see two large smouldering figures stumbling out of the flames. She turned back to the car's console. "Car, top speed to the city centre." She turned to Jaros and said, "They can't possibly track us through the city traffic. Can they?"

As they sped off towards the main road, Jaros mumbled to himself, "Once the Gronch have sensed you they can find you anywhere."

"The what?"

"The Gronch. Those creatures," he repeated.

"What are you talking about? How do you know a name for an alien race? You can add that to the list of things which must be different in the place you come from."

Jaros looked pained for a moment, obviously straining to bring some memories to the surface, and then shook his head. "I don't know, it's just another isolated memory fragment - kind of like remembering that dogs don't like cats, but not being able to remember what dogs and cats actually are."

"And that's all you can remember?"

"Yep, that's it. Doesn't it make you feel all warm and safe knowing that I'm here to rescue you from some creatures which are very definitely called Gronches?"

"It certainly does, but luckily we have a more promising source of salvation," said Kayla, extracting a printout from her other jacket pocket. "Alfred printed this while I was getting up. He said we should do exactly what it says."

"Go on then, read it."

Kayla unfolded the paper and read, "'Drive to the city airport hotel. There you will find a room booked under Jaros' name. Stay at the hotel tonight. Tomorrow morning report to the space departure lounge at 10:15 A.M., where you will find two reservations for the next orbital flight. Wait in the station until you are contacted.'"

"Does it say anything else?" asked Jaros, puzzled.

Kayla checked the back of the paper quickly. "No, that's all there is. What do you think?"

"I think we'll be at the hotel in thirty minutes."

She hesitated. "You don't think it's a bit odd following the instructions of a loony house comp?"

"Why, do you?" returned Jaros.

"No. Mark and I have been doing what Alfred tells us to do for years. When Alfred says to do something, it usually turns out for the best."

The hotel's clerk comp raised one of its plastic eyebrows, "Mr. and Mrs. Smith?"

Jaros grinned sheepishly, "Umm ... yes."

"You are in room 232. Use the lift on your left."

As soon as the doors closed, Kayla burst with laughter.

"What's so funny?" asked Jaros.

"I had a friend who worked on the clerk comps. He said the clerk comps used to be friendly to everyone, but they soon discovered that young couples stopped coming to hotels. It turned out that they didn't really feel naughty unless there was a prudish desk clerk to be shocked at their behaviour!"

The lift doors opened and they found their room. Kayla fumbled with the ID lock for a second. Stepping inside she saw the room was fairly small. Her eyes drifted past the vidscreen console and other furnishings and were drawn to the single large bed. She whispered a thank you to Alfred; he had made the booking and the chances of this being a mistake were close to zero.

"Jaros."

"Yes," Jaros entered the room and followed Kayla's gaze to the bed, and then, realized what had caught her attention, "Oh, there's only one bed. I should go down and ask for a room with two singles."

Kayla had to think quickly, "No, don't bother, it's late. I just want to get some sleep before morning. There's plenty of room for two, and no you can't sleep in the bath, so don't even offer. Besides Alfred was very clear that we must do exactly as the instructions say."

Jaros looked confused. "Why would I want to sleep in the bath?"

"Oh I give up," said Kayla. She started to undress and then stopped for a second to give Jaros the universally understood, 'will you please turn around and stare at that wall' look. Jaros stared back at her for several seconds before taking the hint. "And don't turn back till I say so," she added, just to be sure. When she had finished she climbed into bed, "Okay, you can get in now."

Jaros started to undress, and then realized he was being observed, "You can turn around, too."

"Make me," said Kayla grinning like a Cheshire cat.

Jaros grinned back and said, "Lights out."

Kayla waited in the dark just long enough for someone to take off an item of clothing and was about to say "Lights on" when a pillow hit her squarely in the face. Just as she recovered from that, and was about to try again, a second pillow hit her. At which point she gave up and turned over to sleep.

A minute later Jaros was heard to inquire, "Can I have my pillows back now?"

"Certainly." Thwump.

"Ha, you missed!"

Thwump.

"Jaros."

"I'm asleep."

"You don't think they could track us here, do you?"

Jaros contemplated the question. "Could they find us through the comp networks?" he asked.

"I don't think so. We think the comps gossip among themselves, but we've never caught them at it. Whenever we put a tracer on the communication lines they stop chattering. I doubt anyone could break into the network far enough to trace specific individuals."

"In that case we're probably safe, unless they have some tracking device on one of us or the car."

"Should we post a guard?" asked Kayla.

"No, those creatures would never get through the hotel security systems unnoticed. We'll be woken in plenty of time to escape if they turn up in the hotel lobby."

"Okay, night then," said Kayla.

"You're not going to hit me again?"

"No, probably not. Well, not until you're not expecting it anyway."

"Ok, that's good," said Jaros as he rolled over to attempt to sleep. Instead he ended up lying awake thinking about everything he could remember, trying to remember more, but failing. After a while he heard the sound of regular breathing. Kayla was asleep and he could at last relax, without the fear of being hit again.

Kayla paced back and forth in the spaceport lounge. She'd been growing increasingly jittery as the time for their flight neared.

"Why don't you sit down and relax?" suggested Jaros.

"I can't," Kayla said. "Once we're on that plane we're safe, but until then I keep thinking that any moment those creatures will come barging into the spaceport."

"We'll be boarding in a few minutes. There's nothing to worry about."

"I wish we could talk to Alfred."

"Have you tried plugging him into anything?"

"No, none of the comp plugs I've found match, and I don't want to blow him up by mistake."

"I hope his plan is better than it appears to be. We're going to be pretty well stuck once we get to the orbiting station."

The intercom sounded, "Will passengers on space Flight IX279 please begin boarding at Gate 27."

Jaros checked his ticket, "That's us. Come on." He took Kayla by the hand and they followed some other people who seemed to know where they were going. Kayla was dragging her feet; finally Jaros understood. "You've never been on a space flight before, have you?"

"No."

"You're scared of flying!"

"No, I'm not," she unsuccessfully denied.

"There's nothing at all to be frightened of. It's perfectly safe. If something goes wrong with the drive, they can always glide down to a safe landing. If we get hit by a small meteorite then the walls of the ship automatically reseal as they are filled with a liquid similar to the stuff they put in car radiators."

"I thought you couldn't remember anything! I wish you'd stop talking about it."

"Oh, sorry. I seem to have no shortage of useless facts in my head."

"It's not the flight that scares me. It's the weightlessness."

"Well, in that case I think I can tell you something useful. According to one of the brochures I was reading while you were busy pacing, the station we're going to has a rotational gravity of zero point four G's on the accommodation deck. So, apart from a few minutes of feeling a bit odd while boarding, you won't have anything to worry about."

"Jaros, weightlessness feels just like when you're in a lift and it suddenly starts going down, right?"

"Yep."

"Only worse?"

He nodded. "Yep."

"Well, that makes me feel a bit woozy, so ten minutes of falling while my surroundings appear to be stationary is not going to be my idea of fun."

"But."

Kayla interrupted and locked eyes with him. "Jaros, now would be a good time for you to change the subject, before I become violent."

Jaros took her hand and grinned mischievously. "You know I'll be beside you. If you need to distract yourself from the 'gravity of the situation,' just try to throw something at me. With your aim I'll be almost completely safe."

Kayla laughed. "That is so bad."

"But admit it! You did stop worrying about the trip."

Kayla started to withdraw her hand but paused just before their hands parted and slowly dragged her fingers across the back of his hand. She lowered her voice. "What makes you think I'm distracted by your weak attempts at humour?"

Jaros was too embarrassed to reply and ended up grinning stupidly, trying his best to look unruffled while they waited.

CHAPTER FOUR

A s Jaros predicted, they arrived safely. And although it was difficult, Kayla managed to avoid losing her breakfast in the process. Once safely on the accommodation deck of the station, she began to feel much better. Kayla watched as Jaros made a spectacle of himself by jumping around in the low gravity like a two-year-old on a trampoline. Within a few minutes she'd relaxed enough to see the funny side of things.

"I bet you're one of those people who can eat junk food before going on a roller coaster ride."

"You bet," replied Jaros laughing. "What's a roller coaster?"

"Something I'll show you one day," she promised.

"Great. You know the real secret for getting through something really unpleasant is to look forward to it, and then enjoy the uniqueness of the experience while it lasts, with the firm knowledge that you'll never be stupid enough to get yourself into a similar situation again."

"Cut the two-bit philosophy lesson and take me to lunch. I think I'm getting used to this reduced gravity; and what doesn't make me puke makes me hungry."

Jaros hooked his arm through hers and together they followed the signs to the dining area.

Kayla grinned to herself. She was giving into the strange feelings she was having for him. It really didn't make sense. She had never felt instant attraction to anyone before and it unnerved her more than she cared to admit. Was he feeling the same way? He'd been friendly, even flirty; but was he serious, or just being polite? This was silly. She didn't know why she felt as she did; and yet, she desperately wanted him to feel the same way. Kayla shook her head trying to clear it. Maybe these feelings were normal, but if so, then all of the mushy movies she'd ever seen had totally failed to convey the very thing they were supposed to be about.

"Are you trying to memorize the exits?" asked Jaros.

Kayla was startled from her thoughts and quickly focused on the air lock she was previously staring at with a blank look. "Oh I was wondering what it was," she lied.

"It leads to one of the emergency escape ships. See the sign?" replied Jaros, pointing.

"Do they get used often?"

"I doubt they've ever been used."

The dining room could probably seat thirty or forty people, but it was nearly empty. Kayla sat down and waited at a table while Jaros went to select something to eat. He came back grinning and sat opposite her placing two large plates on the table.

"I'll never eat all that," she exclaimed.

"I thought you were famished. Anyway, I'll finish off anything you don't want."

For the rest of the meal they didn't talk much. Kayla watched Jaros the whole time. Every few mouthfuls he'd look up at her and smile, before resuming his meal.

He'd finished his plate and was halfway through hers when the explosion hit. It felt like the floor fell out from under them. Kayla was twisting about madly until she felt two strong arms catch her. "What's happened?" she shouted to Jaros above the noise of sirens and screams coming from every direction.

"I don't know. This section must have broken loose - we've got to get to that air lock," said Jaros urgently. Kayla's ears felt strange — she was finding it difficult to hear.

He absorbed their momentum with his feet as they hit the ceiling and pushed off towards the corridor in the same movement. Even with Kayla as dead weight, they sailed completely across the room and several feet down the corridor before he had to push off a wall to correct their direction. A second later Kayla found herself inside the air lock door waiting for the pressure to equalize. Her ears continued to pop as the pressure increased. Then the life raft door opened and they drifted out of the air lock and into the raft.

After closing the door, Jaros braced himself against the roof and pushed down on the large lever marked "Release." The lifeboat shuddered briefly as the small craft drifted free.

Kayla floated against one of the walls of the lifeboat - it was quite spacious for two people. Turning, she realized something was wrong with Jaros. He was grimacing.

"What's wrong? Did you hurt yourself when the explosion hit?" asked Kayla, trying desperately to grab on to something to pull herself over to him.

"No, it's not that. I'll be okay in a minute."

"Don't try to fob me off. If you're hurt, then I want to know."

"It's nothing, really. I just wasn't prepared for free fall!"

Kayla studied his slightly green face and eventually caught on with a laugh. "You're feeling space sick because you ate too much!"

Jaros continued examining the tiny raft. "If you've finished being amused, you could help find the radio and turn it on so we can find out what the heck happened to the station."

"I'm sorry. After all, you did rescue me. I would never have gotten to the air lock fast enough alone. Sit here while I find the radio." She then tried unsuccessfully to help him into the chair.

Kayla looked around the room. "Comp?"

"I don't think this lifeboat has one," said Jaros.

"What!" Kayla was speechless. She didn't quite grasp the concept at first. "But... but..."

"You will have to find the radio's manual controls," said Jaros.

Kayla started looking around the ship. She was hampered by her lack of experience with free fall. Her legs kept drifting off in the wrong direction until she could grab hold of something solid to pull them back again. After examining the various knobs and switches on the control panel she said, "I think this is the radio." Pointing to some other knobs she ventured, "And those have something to do with life support. But where are the navigation controls?"

"It's only a lifeboat. I think the nearest thing to a navigation control was that lever I threw when we got on."

"Oh, so we're waiting to be rescued?"

"You bet."

"What if we need to make evasive manoeuvres?"

"To avoid what?"

"Space junk, rocks, I don't know, dangers unknown," she suggested.

"We will have to just rely on luck. Luckily, space is big so we won't need much, unless something actually chases us. Are you ever going to turn that radio on?"

"I'll get to it! I didn't want to blow us up or use up valuable fuel by turning on a rocket motor by accident."

Kayla activated the multi channel radio and was rewarded by a slight hissing sound. She pressed the auto scan button and waited as the numbers flickered by.

...and appear to be under attack. Reports are not clear, but it appears that several of the orbiting stations were hit at approximately 2:15 GMT. At 2:20 GMT one city in China, Europe and U.S.A. was also hit, but the names of the cities have not been released. The extent of casualties is not yet known. The patrol service is refusing to comment on the suggestion that an alien race is responsible for the attack.

The following radio message was received several hours before the attack and may be related:

"This is commander Gudun of the Gronch Empire. If your ruler has not surrendered within two Earth hours, we shall be forced to demonstrate the power of the Gronch Empire."

Civil Defence is warning people not to panic. They advise that reports of large ugly alien creatures roaming the streets are unreliable and simply due to overactive imaginations."

Stay tuned. We will be bringing you up to date with regular reports on the state of the war as new information comes in. For now, we return you to our scheduled programs."

Kayla turned the volume down. "It doesn't make any sense."

"I expect it will, eventually," offered Jaros as he fiddled with the viewing screen. It remained blank until he hit on the right controls; the Earth spun into view, and then disappeared off the other side of the screen. He continued to search around for some time before he managed to find what he was looking for.

The screen showed the broken arm of the station as it rotated slowly with residual spin. Kayla and Jaros floated next to each other, watching it for some time. Kayla steadied herself on Jaros' hand and then kept hold of it.

"Kayla?"

"Yes."

"Now that I've got you alone."

Kayla laughed. "You could have just asked, you know, but I'm touched that you went to so much trouble."

"I thought this would be more dramatic," agreed Jaros.

"So what did you want to say then?"

"Will you marry me?"

Kayla just about choked. "You know, for a minute there I thought you said…"

"I did."

She struggled to get her head around the concept. "You really want to marry me?"

"No, I just wanted to embarrass myself by asking so you could make fun of me."

Kayla smiled, "Oh, that's ok then."

After an awkward silence Jaros prompted, "It's generally considered proper to give an answer of some sort, but don't feel rushed. It's just that I'd hate to die before you make up your mind, and then spend the rest of eternity not knowing if I was an idiot or not. I just figured the way things have been going, I better ask while I've got the chance. If those aliens decide to finish off what they started, it won't be difficult for them to find us with our radio beacon going full blast."

"That's just so romantic!" said Kayla with mock enthusiasm. "I know you are just a male, but you should still realize it's not terribly romantic. I mean, asking to spend the rest of your life with someone seems somehow shallow when that period of time is expected only to be a few minutes."

"Sorry I asked! It's not the situation I would have chosen, but my recent life seems not to be in my control. And although I haven't known you very long, and my memory of the rest of my life is less complete than a Swiss cheese, I still know I've never felt like this before. Whenever you walk in the room, I can barely stop staring at you. When you aren't in the room, I can't stop thinking about the next time I'll see you. When you smile I think the world is a happy place, even when I'm about to die." He smiled and then continued: "And when you laugh at me because I do something stupid, I figure I've briefly made you happy, and life is good and worth suffering through, whatever the cost. And when you don't look happy, I feel sick."

Kayla stared at him, speechless.

"I'm sorry to have embarrassed you, but I wasn't prepared to die without at least saying what I felt. You can consider the matter closed. I'll not mention it again."

"Yes," said Kayla.

"Yes, lets just pretend I didn't open my mouth. We've got enough to worry about in this old lifeboat."

"No, Jaros. I said yes. I said yes to your question."

Jaros would have fallen over if it wasn't for the lack of gravity. "What?"

"I said yes!"

"To the question about spending the rest of our lives together?"

"Yes, that one," she confirmed.

"So you feel…"

Kayla decided to demonstrate as he was clearly having trouble grasping what she was saying. She reached out for his hand and pulled him towards her until their faces were inches apart, then looked deeply into his eyes as their lips slowly met for a kiss.

After some time Jaros gasped, "Okay, I believe you. Let me breathe every once in a while, won't you?" He disengaged himself and started looking round the ship. "We'd better check out the rations and water."

Kayla smiled. "Thinking about your stomach again? Can't I hold your attention for more than a few seconds?"

"Another few seconds and I might have forgotten that I was pretending to be a perfect gentleman. Anyway, I've just decided we'd better survive this."

Kayla found the storeroom. It was the size of a small closet and filled to the ceiling with ration packs. She started sorting through them. "This should put you off your food; we have enough freeze dried packs of vitamin-boosted powder to last six months and every single one is labelled 'Irish Stew.'"

Jaros was playing with the control panel at the front of the ship. "No need to worry about that. Unless I'm reading the wrong gauge, we'll suffocate at least a month before the food runs out."

"Oh, goody!" said Kayla.

Jaros caught motion out of the corner of his eye. "What's that?"

The screen was still showing the broken arm of the space station, but now another craft had appeared. It was bulbous and rusty-coloured. Without the benefit of atmospheric haze, it was impossible to tell its true size until it moved in front of part of the space station.

"Goodies or baddies?" asked Kayla worriedly.

"I don't know. Do you recognize the ship's design?"

"No, but I don't think I would." They watched it together for a few minutes. "I feel like we ought to wave or something."

"Blimey!" exclaimed Kayla, as the ship suddenly shot off the side of the screen.

Jaros was frantically trying to find it again.

"Nothing can accelerate that fast. Can it? All the people inside would have been squashed," she said, frowning.

"It's a fair bet that there weren't any people in it—not humans, anyway." Jaros managed to find it again. It was now stationary, next to a small life raft, presumably another survivor. Nothing happened for a few seconds. Then the life raft silently exploded.

Kayla looked away. She felt cold inside. Jaros' arm pulled her over and he held her tightly. "It's going to another one," said Jaros.

"Are we going to die?" she asked.

"Probably worse."

"What do you mean?"

"They could have hit that life raft without going all the way over to it. I think they're looking for something." He paused, briefly staring at the screen. "Now would be a good time for you to come up with a really brilliant plan," said Jaros.

"There are some space suits in one of those lockers," said Kayla.

"I don't think throwing space suits at them will frighten them away."

"You suggest something, then."

"I guess, since were going to die anyway, we may as well make it difficult for them to find us. And, we may live an extra hour or two."

"We couldn't sabotage their ship as well, could we?"

"Don't know. It's probably not something they would be expecting, a physical assault by two flimsy creatures with no weapons. I say we give it a try."

"Right," said Kayla as she pushed herself over to the locker, pulled out two suits, threw one at Jaros and started putting on the other.

They checked each other's suit carefully. Then Kayla paused, took Jaros by both hands, "I wish we'd had more time."

Jaros stared at her for several seconds, not saying anything, squeezing her hands. Then he grabbed a large pile of Irish stew containers and handed them to Kayla, grinning wickedly, "You'll need some propulsion. Whatever you do, don't let go of me once we're out there. If we get separated, there may not be enough of these stew packets to get us back together again."

Kayla wrapped her arms around his waist and squeezed, "Not a chance. Just let me know if you're having trouble breathing."

"We're going to have to wait here until it comes to check us out. Then I'll make a jump for it. Just hang on tight."

Kayla took a deep breath, her heart hammering with fear, while she waited for the end to come.

CHAPTER FIVE

Jaros clung to the air lock, watching the station debris in the distance. He tried to spot the enemy ship, but without the magnification of the vid screen he couldn't be sure which tiny white dot was which. Even moving relatively slowly, they had already drifted several kilometres away from the bulk of the station.

He continued watching intently, terrified of missing his one chance. Damn, he really didn't want to die now. Kayla was so near; he was having trouble concentrating. He shook himself and then almost let go in fright when a large ugly space ship appeared out of nowhere a few hundred meters away. "Hang on," said Jaros as he dived towards the ship before it could move off or fire.

"Oh great one, the bipedal apes seem to have launched a missile at us."

The alien captain bellowed in response, smashing his large ugly fist against the exceptionally sturdy control panel. "I thought they were too primitive to fight back! They will pay for this insolence."

The bridge became silent as they waited for impact, but nothing happened. The captain looked around at his cowering officers and whispered menacingly: "Somebody had better explain this."

The crew looked around at each other with fear in their eyes, fully aware that one more of their already diminished numbers was more than likely to regret getting up today. A relatively brave, or perhaps stupid, navigation officer piped up, "Sir it appears the missile was, in fact, one of the creatures."

"And how did you deduce this?"

The officer instantly realized his mistake, "I can see the creature now sir. It appears to be trying to damage our garbage disposal unit."

"Do we have any garbage?" asked the captain.

"Yes sir."

The captain burbled happily in anticipation, "Flush it!"

"Yes sir." An officer entered a command code and the ship shook briefly.

"Excellent! Open cargo doors and scoop them up. If you damage them, I will take great pleasure in eating you. If you only damage them a little, I will kill you first."

"Very good, sir. In the event of my failure I do hope you find me to your taste."

Kayla was holding onto one of the handholds – or claw holds – they found, while Jaros tried to damage what he thought was a drive exhaust. Suddenly, the ship shook and the exhaust exploded, knocking Jaros into space. Before she could understand what had happened, something solid hit her head and she found herself spinning slowly in space a few dozen meters from the ship.

Fumbling with her radio controls, she finally got the right button, "Jaros, are you okay?"

Silence.

"Jaros, if you don't answer me I'm never going to speak to you again!"

She waited, but still there was no response. Finally she turned to face the alien ship still only twenty meters away from her. It was coming toward her with large, ugly gaping doors opening before her. Suddenly, she was very, very cross. Finding a decent bloke was hard enough, without man-eating space ships getting in the way. She screamed to herself, "Ghost, if you really exist, I need you... Now!"

When Jaros came around, he was lying on a bed. His head hurt and most of his body was expressing itself painfully.

An attractive, dark-haired young woman leaned over him, "Thank goodness you're alive! What the heck were you doing out there? And why did you go in the first place? It wasn't your mission."

"Who are you?"

She turned to someone else in the room. "How long till the mind block dissolves, Doctor?"

"It should be gone in another few minutes. I'll leave you to look after him until then," said the Doctor as he cleared up to leave.

"Fine, I'll stay with him," she said and sat down to wait.

Jaros suddenly sat bolt upright, "Kayla!"

"Who?" asked the dark haired woman.

"Kayla. We need to go back to get Kayla."

"You mean you weren't alone! That's not good, I don't know if anyone else was picked up. Hold on. I'll check." She stepped over to the comp system and quickly typed a few keys. Her face fell, "I'm sorry, there's nothing here."

Jaros sounded desperate, "Quickly, we need to go back! We didn't have air for long, but there might still be time!"

The woman looked pained. "We can't go back now, and even if we could, it's been almost 8 hours already. I'm sorry, it's too late."

For several minutes Jaros stared at nothing. Then quite suddenly something changed in his eyes. He looked over at the woman, who was still watching him patiently. "Idonea?"

"Yes, Jaros, it's me. I see your memory is returning."

"Yes." Jaros looked around the room, "Where am I? Don't tell me I've been on those darned memory pills again. What was the mission this time? Don't tell me they erased it all. Oh, hells bells! I can't remember anything, except that something important happened. Darn, I can't quite remember. I expect it will come to me soon, unless it's something I'm supposed to forget. I wonder: did the mission go well?"

Idonea shrugged, "I don't know. Sorry."

"That's great," he said, still struggling with his memory. "I wish we didn't have to keep secrets from ourselves so much. It is a bit annoying. So, anything interesting been happening, while I've been gone?"

"Yes. It turns out we're actually engaged now."

Jaros laughed, "Wonderful, did I propose on one..." Halfway through the sentence his mouth fell open and a strange look passed briefly over his face. "Knee?" he finished weakly.

Kayla came around as they removed her helmet. Breathing fresh air, she stared at the men standing beside her. They didn't look like horrible aliens now. Had it all been a dream? What had happened after Jaros was lost? She couldn't remember. Oh cripes, he was really gone; she felt sick in her stomach and almost crumpled.

The man beside her caught her, "Breathe slowly, miss. You didn't suffer much oxygen depravation, but you should take it slowly for the next few minutes."

She looked up at him; his accent and uniform were both strange to her, "Are you with the patrol?"

"The what? Oh them. No, we're…independents. You'll have to ask the captain if you want to know anything else. We were just told to take you to sickbay. The doctor will be in to check on you in a few minutes." They left her lying on the bed in a small, antiseptic room.

Kayla considered getting up to go exploring but thought the better of it and lay back to wait. Soon a grey-haired man appeared wearing the traditional white coat. "I'm sorry to have kept you waiting, but I'm the only medical officer aboard. Since you were conscious, I decided to deal with the other one first."

Kayla froze as her heart did an extra flip and lodged itself in her throat. "Other one? You mean Jaros—is he ok?"

The doctor was a little befuddled. "Did I use his name? I didn't mean to. Oh dear, I do hope I haven't caused any trouble. I can't possibly discuss another patient, and certainly not him of all people! No, no, no! Anyway, he's absolutely fine. You've nothing to worry about. Now, please forget that I mentioned him at all. There's a dear."

Kayla was so relieved. How had he survived? Who cares? He was okay, and she had to see him.

The doctor interrupted her thoughts, "Now, young lady, what's your name and how did you come to be floating around in a space suit?"

She quickly explained the events following the attack on the space station, but left out the personal details and what little she could remember of what happened after they put on the space suits.

While she was talking, she was conscious of the doctor considering her closely. He then examined her arms and legs carefully.

The Doctor then prodded her with various funny-looking instruments and mumbled an occasional, "Ah ha!"

"Will I live?" She asked.

"For as long as the rest of us, but that's no great feat."

"What do you mean?" Her brow creased in puzzlement.

The doctor looked up from his instruments. "Oh, you're from Earth? I guess you wouldn't know."

"Know what?"

"I can't tell you," replied the doctor, as if it was obvious.

Kayla decided to change tactics. "Then, can I see Jaros now?"

"Do you think he would want to see you?"

Kayla smiled to herself. "Yes, I'm fairly sure."

"Interesting. Anyway, no you can't. And for goodness sake stop using his name; the fewer people that know he's on this ship the better."

"Why? What's going on?"

"I have no idea, and that's the way it's supposed to be. Now, stop asking questions that could get us all killed. Meanwhile, I think you can be safely discharged, so I'll send someone to look after you."

Kayla found herself alone and more than a little annoyed. Who were these people? And what was going on?

The face of a girl about Kayla's age, framed with frizzled brown hair, appeared around the door. "Kayla?" she asked before bouncing into the room.

"That's me." Kayla swung herself off the bed.

"Hi, I'm Elan. Are you feeling all right?"

"Yep, fine now," Kayla replied.

"Great, come with me and I'll show you to your room," she added, leading Kayla down the passageway.

"Listen, I really need to know a few things: like where on earth I am and where in heaven we're going, if you'll excuse the puns."

"We're on the *Destiny* bound for Alceron seven."

"Alceron?"

"Our home system. It's about thirty light years from Earth."

"Don't tell me we're going to be there in less than a lifetime of travel."

"Ok, I won't," said Elan, with a large grin on her face.

Kayla waited for an explanation, but none came. "Last I heard there were only two Earth colonies anyway, and neither of them is called Alceron. How do you explain that?"

Elan looked genuinely surprised. "Are you sure?"

"Yep."

"Then I guess we are from one that's unknown. Maybe we should ask the ship comp. It might know more."

That reminded Kayla of something and she started searching her pockets. "Alfred's gone!"

"Who?"

"My comp. I had him on the life raft. I've been carrying him around with me."

"Maybe you dropped him when they took you out of your suit. We can check later if you want."

Kayla wanted to go and look straight away, but Elan insisted they settle her into her quarters first.

Elan led her into a small cabin. It had barely enough room for two bunks. Everything else was currently folded away within the walls. "We're sharing. I hope you don't mind."

"No, that's fine." Kayla paused, trying to decide if Elan was really the friend she appeared to be. "Elan, I am a little bit lost. I don't know what's going on and I need to find Jaros. And, while we're at it, I'd like to know something about him; you all seem to know who he is."

"You don't know? Oh, I suppose you wouldn't, being from Earth."

"No I don't, and if you fob me off with another, 'I can't tell you,' I'll scream."

"Well, I don't know much apart from the obvious. I don't know him personally. He's slightly unreal, like this mission to Earth. He wasn't supposed to go at all, but he took the place of the original agent and risked his own life. He's just a hero personality, I guess. It's such a pity he's taken."

Kayla suddenly felt ill, "What do you mean, taken?"

"Apparently he and Idonea Karvelas are official. They often compete at the games and there's been gossip for years, especially when they danced together at last year's palace ball. I thought it was all just talk until the papers announced their engagement last week. Frankly, I'm not fond of Idonea. She's a spoilt brat, if you ask me; and I'm not just saying that because I'm jealous, which I am. I was in a class with her once, years ago; maybe she's grown up since then. I hope so for his sake."

Kayla hadn't really heard much of what Elan had been saying. Her brain had stalled trying to cope with Jaros being alive but not available. Why did she care so much? Why was it hurting so much?

Elan noticed the unfocused look on Kayla's face and took the hint. "Maybe you need to rest. You've been through a lot. I'll pop in and wake you before dinner."

Kayla nodded silently, managing something resembling a smile as Elan left. Then she returned to her thoughts.

It was a risk not knowing anything about Jaros' past, but for some reason it didn't seem important at the time. Now it was too late. Now she was stuck, hopelessly in love with someone who was not available. Damn, this wasn't acceptable. Maybe it would be easier if she could blame him. Hate would hurt less than this. It was definitely a good idea, but she didn't hate him.

Up until now, nothing that happened had really mattered, as long as Jaros was there. Now it all came clearly back to her. She was on a ship with people she didn't know, running from alien creatures which wanted to kill her, or worse, and she had effectively lost touch with everyone she'd ever been close to. She was alone! And there wasn't anything she could do about it. Frustrated and angry, she punched the wall with her hand, "Ouch, now my hand hurts too!"

CHAPTER SIX

"Wakey, wakey! Dinner's in twenty minutes," said Elan brightly.

Kayla opened her eyes and felt some of Elan's good mood brushing off on her, despite her own feelings. "How many people at dinner?"

"About thirty."

"Then I need a shower. Is there time?"

"Sure, and if you want to borrow some clothes, just take anything you like from the closet."

"Thanks."

"The shower is in there," said Elan, pointing to what looked like a small closet.

Stripping off her clothes, Kayla stepped in and closed the door.

"Please specify intensity, duration and temperature," said the comp.

"The works, please."

"That is not a predefined setting. Please be more specific."

"Just give me a normal shower, okay?"

The not-very-bright comp got the idea and started the shower. Kayla stood still, enjoying the jets of hot water on her skin.

The shower stopped all too quickly and Kayla reluctantly stepped out into the empty room. On one of the beds was a large soft towel, several sets of clothing, and a note from Elan saying she'd be back to collect her in a couple of minutes.

Revising her view of the world, Kayla decided that she did have a friend, after all. She was just checking her eyes for redness in the mirror when Elan reappeared.

"Wow! Knockout," said Elan.

"Thanks; you're not bad, either," said Kayla, smiling.

Elan looked a little embarrassed. "Come on, or we'll be late. I'm starving."

The dining hall was bustling with people. The crew looked more like vacationers than the military personnel Kayla had expected. There were two long tables with a shorter table crosswise at one end that appeared to be reserved for special guests or higher ranks. Elan directed her through the self-service line and then lead her to one of the longer tables.

Red and gold drapes hung around the walls. The tables were covered with fine silverware. Kayla thought the room looked more like a banquet hall from romantic times of old than the mess level of a star ship.

They were sitting near the end of one of the long tables farthest from its head. Elan pointed out various notables as they arrived.

A tall, thin, middle-aged man with dark hair entered the room accompanied by a tall, attractive, dark-haired young woman. They sat at the short table with the other VIPs. "That's the prince's chief advisor, Ranic Karvelas, with his daughter, Idonea. Normally, the captain would sit where Ranic is sitting, but he's probably on watch."

"Your planet has a monarchy?"

"Of course. It's the only way, don't you think?" Elan was about to say something else, but she was stopped mid-word as silence descended on the room. Ranic stood at the head table. "Please be upstanding and give thanks for the safe return of our prince."

Trumpets blasted from the sound system as doors behind the head table opened and the prince majestically entered, followed by a large metallic robot.

For a moment, Kayla's professional eyes were reflexively drawn to the unusually constructed robot. Then she looked at the prince and her mouth fell open. It was Jaros!

Elan whispered in her ear: "You really know the prince?"

Kayla was watching Jaros limp in to take his place between Idonea and Ranic.

Jaros stood formally for a moment, "I should be thanking you, Lord Ranic, as you have not only held things together in my absence, but also rescued me from the jaws of death." He turned to the rest of the room and lifted his glass, "May the Gronch Empire fall quickly!"

Kayla was almost certain she'd caught his gaze during the toast, but he hadn't appeared to recognize her. Anyway nothing else really mattered now, he was alive! But she sensed that something was seriously wrong. Damn him! She wasn't so needy that she couldn't wait for a more private moment to talk. She turned to Elan and whispered, "Tell me more about these memory blocks?"

"Ssh! You're not even supposed to think about stuff like that. I'll tell you later."

"Cool." Looking around the room Kayla spotted something that had been bothering her. "How come practically no one else is talking?"

"It's considered good practice to stick to telepathy, if at all possible."

"Oh," said Kayla.

CHAPTER SEVEN

Sleep wasn't coming easily. Kayla tossed and turned as quietly as she could, then stared at the ceiling a bit. She had been so busy trying to watch Jaros while pretending not to, that she hadn't eaten enough. Elan was asleep in the other bed. Kayla quietly got out of bed, pulled on a robe and tiptoed out into the passage.

She still didn't know her way about but figured that the galley would be somewhere near the dining room.

There were three sets of doors leading out of the dining room: the doors Kayla had just come through, the ones Jaros had entered through earlier during the banquet and some others on the side. Kayla chose the latter by a process of elimination. Sure enough she found herself in the ship's galley.

It was clearly designed for producing large quantities of food but also very compactly arranged, as everything aboard a ship must be. Kayla found the fridge and was considering which of the many leftovers to start with, when a hand tapped her on the shoulder. She twisted around in fright, stumbling against the fridge door in the process.

"I didn't mean to startle you," said a large, roundly built gentleman.

"Sorry, it was my fault. I didn't eat much at dinner, so I was just looking for a little snack. You don't mind, do you?"

"No, not at all. I missed dinner and had a similar plan myself. Perhaps you'll do me the honour of joining me for a quick bite? I do hate to eat alone."

Kayla's heart rate was beginning to come down after the horrible feeling of being caught with her hand in the proverbial cookie jar. "I'd love to."

"Great. My name's Breckin," he said, as he selected a sizeable number of items from the fridge. Kayla could tell she was in the hands of an expert and simply tried to help carry the booty to the table.

"I'm Kayla."

"Oh, no wonder I didn't recognize you. You're the one we picked up with Jaros," he said.

"Yes, that would be me."

"How are you finding life aboard ship?" he asked, while handing Kayla an enormous sandwich.

"Pretty comfortable, so far. This is great," she said, taking a large bite. "I'm still a little confused about a few things though."

"I'm afraid that's a way of life for Alceronians. We have a lot of secrets, or I've heard we do, but no one will tell me for certain. Now that the war's begun for real, I guess some of the secrets won't be necessary anymore." He paused, taking an enormous bite of his sandwich.

Kayla prompted him to continue. "With whom are we at war?"

"Ah, that I do know: the Gronch Empire. They are a very nasty lot. Our strategy so far has been to hide from them, but that isn't going to work any longer. The trouble is they have mental powers, which make any normal attack almost impossible. It also makes keeping a secret from them rather tricky."

"You mean they're telepathic?"

"Of course, with Calron's help we can match their technology. Although, it's taken years to develop mental abilities and we still don't come near to their ruler's mental powers."

"How come I've never heard of all this before?" inquired Kayla.

"Well, it wouldn't have been much of a secret if everyone had known, would it? Anyway, stop asking questions and start eating; you've hardly got any meat on you," he said, eyeing her arms disapprovingly.

"I'm just fine the way I am, thank you very much. In fact, you could do with losing a bit of weight actually."

He grinned, then patted his rounded stomach, "Rubbish, girl! There's nothing wrong with carrying around a bit of reserve for an emergency," he replied, finishing off another chicken leg.

Kayla started tidying things away, "Thanks for answering my questions. Most people clam up as soon as I ask a question, muttering something about having to check with the captain. No one will do anything without checking with the silly captain first. He must be some kind of ogre, I expect."

"Yes, I expect I am, but mostly people don't call me that to my face."

The plate Kayla was carrying fell into the sink prematurely. "Oops!"

"I rather gathered you were under some sort of misunderstanding," he said, trying not to laugh.

"It's not funny. You could have let on."

"I don't like to brag."

Spying a cloth in a bucket under the sink, she threw it at him. "Wipe that grin off your face."

"Mutiny, eh?"

"Nope! It doesn't count. I'm passenger, not crew."

"Oh, bother, I guess you've got me there," he replied while wiping down the table. "Heads up!" he yelled before tossing the wet cloth back at Kayla, and diving out the door before she could return fire.

"I'll get you later," she shouted after him.

She finished cleaning up and headed back to her room feeling much the better for the meeting. Some parts of the puzzle were starting to make sense now.

Graator watched from his elevated platform in the middle of a dimly lit room. The walls were a soothingly dark green colour and hidden sprays ensured they remained permanently damp. A young battleship commander entered the room. Graator scanned his mind but found nothing exceptional. "Commander Gudun, report at once on your mission," Graater ordered.

"It was not a complete success sir; we were initially obstructed by their primitive society. The first few human subjects we captured didn't seem to know who their leader was."

"What do you mean? How could that be?"

"I don't know sir. We questioned and tortured them and scanned their weak minds, but almost every subject gave a different answer."

Graater's face curled into a hideous shape that might have been some kind of frown. "Did you track down any of these supposed leaders?"

"Yes, Sir. Although several of them proved impossible to find, a number of them referred to a being called 'God,' but their descriptions of his nature and whereabouts differed. We did manage to find several creatures referred to as presidents, a couple of kings, and a pope. But none of them had any mental abilities worth mentioning. Some of the subjects insisted that they were ruled by groups of individuals elected by popularity. I thought these groups may constitute some sort of mental gestalt, but investigation revealed their group mentality was considerably sub normal to the rest of the population when taken as individuals, hard to believe as that may be."

Quickly growing impatient, Graator inhaled deeply expanding his bulbous body. "So you completely failed to find their leader?"

Gudun took a step backwards in fear. He wanted at least to finish his report before being destroyed, but fleet commanders had been killed for much lesser failures. "But sir, I think we did track down their leader. I ordered our telepaths to search for a powerful mind, and they eventually succeeded. I sent down three of my best Gronch warriors to capture the creature, but they failed. One of them was killed in the attempt, and the other two I destroyed personally upon their return."

The Gronch leader started to turn a darker shade of green. "So, you lost three good Gronch and allowed a primitive alien creature to escape?"

Gudun desperately tried to continue his report, knowing that its completion would coincide with his demise. "I think they may not be as primitive as they at first appeared. We made a punitive attack on their small world to demonstrate the foolishness of resistance. Several of our attack craft were destroying survivors — as is normal practice — when I received a distress call from one of our small craft. It was under attack and before they could describe the attacking ship the transmission ceased. Our sensors picked up evidence of a non-Gronch designed anti-matter drive in the vicinity. We traced it leaving the system."

"You know its destination system?"

"Yes, sir. We think so."

Graator relaxed and let his skin resume its former shade of green, although he felt a little peeved at missing out on the fun of a little death and destruction. Good help was hard to come by these days, so he couldn't afford to waste a partially competent officer. "You've done well, Gudun. Could it have been a Silinian ship?"

"No, sir. The traces didn't match a Silinian type drive."

"I want you to take a couple of battle cruisers and capture this alien ship. If you perform well, there could be a promotion in this for you."

Gudun felt his leg joints shaking a little as he left.

Elan was up and gone by the time Kayla awoke. Kayla took another shower before dressing. The door slid open just as she was wondering what to do.

"Kayla, you're up at last. I tried to wake you earlier, but you seemed to be enjoying your sleep too much," said Elan, cheerfully entering the room. "I've got great news. The captain has ordered that I am to start training you full time, which means I get out of all of my normal, dull duties."

"Training at what?"

"MT, telepathy, and other skills, too."

"Really?"

"Yes, but don't get your hopes up too high. Only a small percentage of humans have latent MT abilities."

"But I thought you said last night that everyone was talking to each other telepathically?" Then another thought struck Kayla, "You are humans?"

Elan laughed, "Of course we are, but we weren't picked at random, and we've all been practicing since birth."

"So my chances are pretty slim."

"Not too bad. It's a lot easier to learn when one of the two people already knows what they're doing.

That's why experiments almost always failed on Earth. Even in the rare cases where both subjects had latent ability, the chance of both of them doing the right thing to make the communication work was practically nil."

"How do we start?"

Producing a small gadget attached to a headset with some dangling wires, Elan said, "The first thing is to get control of your mind. We'll start with a few feedback exercises."

Elan attached the headset and let Kayla hold the display. "In this mode it gives a simple cross-section display of your mind. The brighter areas show those parts of your brain that are working."

The display showed exceptional detail, with small areas flickering brighter and paler within fractions of a second.

Elan pointed to the brighter area at the back, "This is the area dealing with what you're seeing. And these areas on the sides are processing audio input. See how they flicker as I talk? This area is where language gets processed; it's also flickering while I talk."

It was kind of eerie to see her own mind ticking over. Kayla experimented by closing one eye expecting one side to go dimmer, but instead both sides dimmed partially.

"Your eyes are connected to both sides of your brain, the left eye goes to the right half of your brain and visa versa," explained Elan. "Now, I want you to just experiment with this for a while. Most of your brain isn't under conscious control, it just works away merrily on its own, but with practice you should be able to get most areas to change in brightness, just by thinking the right thoughts. I'll leave you alone so you can concentrate. I'll be back in a half an hour to see what you can do."

"How do I know when I'm doing it right? Is there a test?"

"No, you just have to try and get control over it," said Elan. Then she remembered something. "When we were young we used to try and make a picture appear, something simple like a face or a tree — you can try that, if you want."

"Okay," laughed Kayla, "I'll try that, if I get bored."

By the end of the day Kayla was sick of practicing. Elan had shown her the settings for practicing different things, but none of them seemed to have anything to do with telepathy. Elan didn't seem to be paying attention, so Kayla started thinking about Jaros. She wanted to go to see him, but she didn't dare. Now that he had his memory back he might not feel the same way any more. Besides, she couldn't just waltz in and confront him, could she?

Elan jumped off the bed, interrupting Kayla's daydreaming, "Come on! Idonea is playing Graeme in the recreation room. If we're not quick, we won't be able to get in."

"Who's playing what?" asked Kayla.

"Come on," said Elan, pulling Kayla off the bed and dragging her down the passageway. "The recreation room isn't very big and anyone else who isn't on duty will want to watch."

When they arrived the room already appeared to be full, but Elan pulled her in and they squeezed through until they could see the game board. The board was nearly a meter square, covered with about twenty small shiny objects of two different colours, each one about the size of a button. The room was completely silent despite the number of people. Kayla waited expecting Idonea or her opponent to move one of the objects, but neither of them did anything. Idonea's opponent was a man in his early thirties, thin with greying hair. He had sweat running down his brow. Kayla was still trying to remember whether or not he was one of the people Elan had pointed out to her at the banquet when she caught something moving out of the corner of her eye.

"They're moving!" Kayla whispered involuntarily and immediately wished she hadn't. Everyone turned and looked at her as if she were brain-damaged.

The pieces were moving very slowly over the board, some faster than others. The changing pattern was entrancing, but Kayla began wondering about what the game's objective was.

Her eyes strayed to the players. They were both completely motionless, with concentration clearly showing on their faces. Kayla hadn't been this close to Idonea before. She took the chance to examine her closely. She had to admit, Idonea was pretty, but only in a cold, emotionless way. Graeme was quite handsome, with just enough grey hair to lend a distinguished appearance. There seemed to be something funny about his left arm, but from this angle it was hard to see what.

Suddenly, a tiny blue spark started flickering between two pieces. After a few seconds the piece being attacked backed away, but before it could make good its escape, it encountered two more of the green pieces. The blue sparks continued for a few more seconds before the tiny piece faded from bright red to white. By this time, other battles were taking place between green and red pieces around the board. Kayla watched in silence, while everyone else tried to keep track of the action.

The game continued for another fifteen minutes before a clear winner began to emerge. There were only three or four green pieces still playing, when Graeme relaxed his stern expression and stood up. When he stood, Kayla realized his left sleeve was empty.

"I concede, you've got me again," said Graeme.

"You played well today, Graeme. Losing an arm seems to have sharpened your mind; perhaps all officers should have a limb removed," said Idonea, laughing at her own sense of humour.

Several of the spectators gave her distinctly unpleasant looks. Kayla wondered whether Idonea was actually feeling the thoughts that seemed to be darting about the room. The atmosphere was thick enough to cut with a knife. Graeme excused himself politely and left. The rest of the spectators dispersed fairly quickly. It seemed like no one wanted to be the last person left in the room with Idonea. Kayla and Elan escaped with the rest of the crowd.

"Did he lose his arm recently?" Kayla asked as soon as they were alone.

"Yes. He got a leak in his suit while making repairs to a ship and his arm froze before he could get back inside. Without the shoulder seals he would have died."

"Is Idonea like that with everyone?"

"Yes. She's not actually a bad person, just incredibly cold. Such a waste, really; she's got an excellent mind."

"How does the game work?" Kayla asked, changing the subject.

"You mean Stragaw?"

"Yes."

"Each piece has a miniaturized motor and control lever inside. They pick up electrical energy from an alternating field built into the board. The colour on top gives a reading of how fully charged each piece is. Red pieces are charged positively and green pieces negatively. When they come within a few millimetres of each other the charge starts to arc between the two pieces."

"Killing both if it's one-on-one and they're equally charged?"

"Yep. But, if it's two-on-one then the two still have some charge left when the one runs out. They recharge again slowly from the board as long as they haven't run out completely."

"But how is their movement controlled?"

"That's the main part of the game. It's designed to improve strategy and give mind control exercise at the same time. Each piece has a tiny lever inside, which determines its direction of travel. To make the pieces move, you just have to move the lever with your mind. The lever is very sensitive, so it doesn't take much; but most people get exhausted from the effort. To win, you have to avoid any unnecessary moves."

"Doesn't that make the game very uneven, if one person has a more powerful mind?"

"No more than chess is unfair if one person is brighter than another. In fact, it sometimes evens things out. For instance Graeme is much better at strategy than Idonea, but he can't afford to make nearly as many direction changes with his pieces. They usually play a very close game."

After a long morning of fruitless exercises, Kayla was returning from the galley with enough snacks to keep them both going for the rest of the day when Jaros walked around the corner, nearly bumping into her.

For several long seconds they stood facing each other. "Hello," she said, awkwardly.

"Kayla?" he blurted, as if he had just demonstrated some wonderful feat of mental gymnastics just to get her name right.

Kayla was getting cross. "Oh, don't bother. If it's that hard, you can just forget the whole thing. I wouldn't dream of holding you to your promise."

"What...?" started Jaros, but Idonea came around the corner.

"Hello," she interrupted. "I don't think we've met. Are you the girl we rescued?"

"Apparently, yes," replied Kayla.

"So," said Jaros, "has someone been looking after you?"

"Yes. I'm being looked after just fine, and they've been trying to teach me some of this mind stuff, but I'm afraid it all appears to be fairly hopeless."

"Oh, you poor dear," said Idonea. "I'd forgotten you were an Earth girl. How do people live when they can't communicate more than a few feet from each other?"

Kayla gave Idonea a withering stare and said, "Luckily, someone invented the vidcom a few years back. You should try it."

"Oh, yes, I've heard Earth people rely on that sort of thing. It's sort of like a crutch for a cripple, isn't it Jaros?"

"Ah, yes," replied Jaros, taking Idonea by the hand. "Come on Idonea, I've got to get back to the bridge. Why don't you walk me?"

"It's been lovely meeting you Kayla. You must keep trying with your psycho-tech lessons, even if there isn't really any hope," Idonea called back.

Then Jaros turned back briefly and winked.

Kayla stood speechless for a full minute. She didn't know what to do. She had been about ready to bop Idonea; instead, she hurried back to her room and made do quietly fuming and thinking of all the nasty things she might do to Idonea and Jaros. It wasn't nearly as satisfying as actually doing them, but a great deal more socially acceptable.

Elan came in carrying a small board about four centimetres square with one of the small Stragaw pieces on it. "Here is a Stragaw trainer. It's got an extra sensitive control so the slightest stray psychokinetic energy will set it going."

"Humph," said Kayla, still angry and upset.

"What's wrong?"

Kayla said nothing for a few seconds and then decided to confide in Elan. "If I tell you, you have to promise never to repeat it."

"I promise," said Elan with interest.

"Cross your heart and hope to die?"

"Yes, yes. Stop stalling and give."

"Well, you know how I was picked up with Jaros?"

"Yes."

"Well, we'd been together for a while before that. He was staying with me on Earth, and we'd gotten quite close."

"You didn't?"

"No!" said Kayla, pretending to be shocked, and thought to herself: 'not for want of trying on my part, anyway.'

"When we were on the lifeboat and it looked like we were going to die… "

"You pledged your undying love for one another!" interrupted Elan jokingly.

"Basically, yes."

Elan's eyes bulged, "You're kidding!"

"He proposed."

"No!"

"And I accepted."

"But he's engaged to Idonea."

"Well I didn't know that then, and neither did he!"

"Cripes! Have you asked him how he feels now?"

"Well I haven't actually asked, no. I've only spoken to him once since, a few minutes ago."

"So… What did he say?"

"I don't know. He really didn't say anything, now that I think about it, nothing specific. It was almost as though he didn't want me to say anything either; the vibes just didn't make sense."

Jaros was struggling with his memory still. It was coming back now, in bits and pieces. It shouldn't be, he was sure, but seeing Kayla had jolted almost everything back. He still had gaps, but he knew what happened between them now, and he wanted to see Kayla to find out what was going on in her head. But he couldn't risk it at the moment.

"Calron, have you had any ideas of who could have sent me that note?"

The silvery robot turned its head a few degrees to face Jaros. "No, I haven't. I still don't see how you could have thought I would send you a note telling you to take over a mission from an agent we've been training for months. You were very lucky to get back in one piece. I do wish you humans would stop and think on occasion."

"Yes, I realize now how stupid it was. Please don't keep going on about it. At least it meant I got to meet Kayla. I bumped into her this morning. I think I should talk to her, whatever the risk."

"Don't worry about Kayla; I've made sure she will be kept busy and out of harm's way. The further from you she is, the safer she will be. And the less she knows, the safer we all are."

"But I don't have to like it!"

The robot turned slowly away. Its impassive face betrayed nothing of its thoughts. Whether it cared or not would never be known, at least not by any creature as simple as a human.

The piece continued to do nothing.
"Just concentrate. It's not that difficult."
"I am concentrating."

"Let's start again. First relax. Take a couple of deep breaths."

Kayla released the bedclothes she clenched in her fingers and took a deep breath.

"Now, start to concentrate on the piece, look only at the piece until everything else in the room starts to fade from view," instructed Elan. Continuing a few seconds later she said, "When that one piece stands all on its own, try to push."

Kayla's face was all screwed up with the effort. Still, nothing happened.

"I've got to go to check the duty roster; you keep trying. It might be easier while I'm not in the room."

After a few minutes, Kayla collapsed back on the bed. It was hopeless; nothing she did would make it move.

She had to learn how to do this stuff so Idonea couldn't look down on her. Thinking of Idonea made her angry. She would like to see her ghost give Idonea a good fright.

"Oh well, I'd better keep at it," Kayla said to herself, sitting up to try again.

The board was empty. Looking around, Kayla finally spotted the piece chugging along happily underneath the bed.

Kayla didn't believe it at first. After making no progress for days, it was hard to believe she had succeeded. She took the piece back, reset it, and placed it back in the middle of the board.

Another few minutes of fruitless effort convinced her it was either a malfunction in the piece or a stray psychokinetic field from someone else on the ship.

"Had any success?" said Elan, when she came back in.

"I'm not sure," replied Kayla.

"What happened?"

"I was concentrating and nothing was happening, so I lay back to rest for a minute. When I looked back, the piece had started moving. But I haven't been able to get it to move again since."

"Are you doing the same things?"

"Yes, just like you showed me."

"What about your thoughts? What were you thinking about when it started moving?"

"I don't know; it must have started moving while I was relaxing. I was thinking about Idonea and—" Kayla stopped as a thought suddenly struck her.

"And what?"

"And...Jaros," she lied.

"Try thinking about them again."

Kayla looked down at the little piece and asked her Ghost to give it a very gentle push.

The piece immediately started chugging across the board at high speed.

"Wow!" exclaimed Elan, clearly impressed. "Now put the headset back on and switch to the mind view."

Kayla obediently put the head set on.

"Now, watch the screen and think about Jaros and Idonea again, like you did before."

Ignoring Elan's instructions, Kayla asked her Ghost to push the piece again. Sure enough, it changed direction.

"See that area there, it brightened just before the piece turned. All you have to do now is practice with the vid screen, until you can control that part of your mind at will; then we can start work properly. Telepathic control will probably be fairly close to that area, so practice with anything that brings results around about there."

CHAPTER EIGHT

"Father, I'm worried about the battle; I know you promised me I'd lead our forces, but sometimes I think I may not be the right person for the job."

"Leave your problem with me, Idonea. I'll sort something out."

"Thanks," she said, much relieved.

As the door slid shut, Ranic cursed silently. He really had no intention of letting her control the fleet in a real battle, but he couldn't very well tell his own daughter that.

He turned his mind to the girl who had come aboard with the prince. She was still an unknown entity. Her mind had a strange opaque quality to it. She either had very good mind control or no mental ability at all. He favoured the latter as it was entirely more common and would simplify things a great deal. Yet, something about her worried him.

Down in a passage near the Engineering Room, Calron's metallic form leaned against the wall. A couple of officers walked past and saluted him. When they were gone, he continued his interrupted conversation with a muffled voice coming through a slit in the wall. "It's okay, they have passed. Things are going well; we should be at Alceron in another day or two."

"Do you think anyone suspects?"

"No, we have them all fooled."

"Good. It's sneaky, but necessary. Continue with the plan we've outlined, but for goodness' sake keep an eye on both of them."

"Yes, sir."

Kayla lay on her bed looking at the ceiling. She was still a little shaken. All her life she'd believed something was watching over her, and now, it turned out to have been her own subconscious all along. The realization also meant that she was responsible for causing certain happenings, when she had thought she was simply an innocent bystander. Still, the Nun at the orphanage shouldn't have shouted at Mark like that. She had deserved it.

With the help of the vid screen and brain scanner, Kayla had the tiny piece under perfect control within a few hours. Elan seemed suitably impressed with her progress. A couple of times Kayla pushed a little too hard and the piece had flipped over. Elan seemed to think this was due to some malfunction in the piece. Kayla didn't bother to correct her misinterpretation.

The door slid open and Captain Breckin poked his head in. "How is our newest recruit doing?" he asked.

Elan snapped to attention. "Progressing well, sir."

Kayla looked up and smiled. "I see you haven't lost any weight since we last met."

Elan's eyes popped a little at hearing someone speak to the captain like that.

"I see you haven't gained any," replied Breckin, before turning to Elan, "Sit down and relax girl—you don't want Kayla thinking I'm some kind of ogre, do you?"

"No, sir," she said, trying to sound relaxed.

"I came to see if you would like the ten-cent tour of the ship."

"I'd love it. I'm still getting lost all the time."

"Okay, come on then. You too, Elan, and try not to walk at attention."

"Yes, sir. I mean, no, sir."

"How big is the ship?" asked Kayla.

"It's a sphere with a diameter of thirty meters, ten levels and an average of about fifteen rooms on each level, nearer twenty in the middle levels and only two or three near the top or bottom. A sphere gives the maximum internal volume for a minimum of the expensive outer surface."

"You use a standard reaction less matter – anti matter drive?"

"Yes, it's in the middle of the ship. The particles are created and then accelerated in the opposite direction in which we want to go. Then they are brought together to annihilate each other, producing energy used to create more matter – anti matter particles."

They stepped into an elevator, which shot them rapidly to the top level of the ship. Kayla was reminded of the unpleasantness of weightlessness.

"Doesn't that break a few rules of physics?" asked Kayla, who hadn't heard it described before.

"Not half as many as the inertia-less system does. The anti matter drive is really just pushing against space itself, but the inertia-less drive manages to cut the sphere containing the ship right out of normal space, so its inertia relative to real space no longer exists. Then, the only limit to speed is a complex relationship between the size of the ship and the size of the drive. Internally, we still feel the acceleration as if it was the normal one or two G's that the drive produces. But externally, we go from stationary to a respectable multiple of the speed of light in no time flat. Which is about the same as disappearing."

Elan followed along meekly, still finding it hard to reconcile this talkative good-humoured man with the captain with whom, for weeks, she had been in awe. She had started to feel much more self-confident acting as Kayla's teacher, but at times like this she remembered how lucky she was to have secured a place on the *Destiny* at all.

They continued through various levels of the ship, Breckin pointing out the mechanical niceties which Kayla not only dutifully admired but in which she displayed a genuine interest.

Jaros was pacing the bridge. He was the officer on watch. This consisted of sitting in a chair and waiting for an emergency to arise. Most of the time nothing happened and it became rather dull, particularly so during the wee small hours of the morning.

The bridge was housed near the middle of the ship quite close to the anti matter drive and the inertia less field generator. There were six large vid screens across the front of the bridge, each showing one of the six views: forward, aft, port, starboard, zenith, and nadir, but only when the ship was well below light speed. They were arranged like an unfolded cube, with four of the screens in a cross and the rear view on the right hand side. Jaros occasionally glanced up at the vid screens, which showed a computer-generated view of any stars that would have been visible if there were any windows. Even at the speed they were going, nothing ever moved, unless they happened to pass dangerously close to a star system.

Jaros sat down and was staving off sleep when the door slid open and the captain entered, followed by Kayla and Elan. He tried to pretend he'd been fully alert and aware of their approach.

"This is supposedly the centre of operations, although you can see our prince isn't exactly being run off his feet at the moment," Breckin said to the girls, the slightest smirk stretched across his face.

Jaros flashed a big grin at both of the girls and both of them smiled back; then Kayla turned away and made a show of ignoring him for the rest of the bridge tour. Strange, he thought to himself. Something was clearly wrong. He decided to go to see her the next chance he got.

CHAPTER NINE

*K*ayla didn't like to do it, but she was sick of being fobbed off. As Breckin escorted them both back to their room she invited him in, carefully moved around behind him, and pressed the button to close and lock the door.

"I want to know what the hell is going on. I've been attacked in my home, attacked in space, picked up and ignored for the best part of a week by a ship from a planet that doesn't exist populated by a bunch of people who won't tell me anything. You're not leaving here until I get some answers."

The captain had a bemused look on his face. Elan was obviously speechless.

"A fiery wench, I'll warrant. You don't really think you can stop me from leaving?" asked Breckin, comparing her slight frame to his own generous proportions.

"You'd be surprised. Start talking or try leaving; no other options are available."

He paused, looking thoughtful for a few seconds, then jumped towards Kayla. She sidestepped neatly, grabbing him around the neck from behind. Quickly, he stepped backwards and began to fall, letting his weight carry them down to the ground, where Kayla was forced to release her hold and roll aside to avoid being squashed.

Kayla sprang up ready for another attempt, but relaxed when she saw Breckin was incapacitated with laughter.

"I should never live it down if any of the men find out—brought down by a wee slip of a girl. You wrestle well."

"Thank you."

Breckin at last managed to regain his self-control. "Anyway, I'm perfectly happy to tell you what I know. Unfortunately it's not a lot."

"But you're the captain!"

"And, therefore, in a perfect position to be captured. You know about the Gronch. They attacked you on Earth and then again in space. They are the ruthless rulers of a good number of local systems. We knew that sooner or later they would find Earth, if they didn't already have agents watching it. So, a plan was devised to enable us some day to defeat them. Since they are telepathic the plan had to be kept secret, even from our own people."

"Go on," encouraged Kayla.

"That's about it. The plan is still a secret. All I know is that a mission needed to be performed on Earth, which is what we came for. I don't even know if the mission was successful."

"But someone must know what's actually going on."

"No, not anyone as far as I know—except Calron, of course. It's his plan."

"Who exactly is this Calron person?"

"He's not a person; he's a computer of sorts. But that's another story," said Breckin, jumping briskly to his feet and out the door before Kayla could react.

They found themselves alone again. "I don't know that we actually found out much. I still don't know who Calron is, or, more importantly, what all this has to do with me."

"But we did find out one thing about you."

"What?"

"That you've got clearance from Calron. The captain wouldn't have told you anything otherwise. It also explains why we haven't had any luck with telepathy yet."

"How do you figure that?"

"Most people have little or no telepathic abilities. With those people the technique is to try and get their mental processes working. Some rare individuals have lots of mental ability, but they also have a natural mental block to prevent their thoughts from leaking out to everyone they walk past. The fact that Calron trusts you to keep what you know a secret means that you are almost certainly in the latter category, so we can change our methods to break down those barriers."

"No time like the present. What do we do?"

"Come over here."

Kayla sat cross-legged on the bed facing Elan. They held hands as they had done on previous attempts.

"Start by relaxing your mind as completely as possible. It will be easier if you are close to the state just before sleep. If you start to feel something, then play with those parts of your mind you've been working on. Try to increase the feeling."

Kayla relaxed as she'd been taught to do, clearing her mind and counting down from ten, making each number sound a little slower and deeper in her mind.

For a few minutes nothing seemed to happen. Elan's eyes were closed and her face showed the effects of concentration. Finally, a slight tickling sensation began. Kayla tried to help it and it stopped, so she relaxed and it started again. This time she made it stronger. The room was little more than a blur to Kayla; her eyes were open, but they saw nothing. The feelings in her head were increasing and the bed seemed to be shaking.

At one point Kayla accidentally cut the feeling off for a second and Elan cried out, but it came back again even stronger.

"Can you hear me?"

Kayla felt pain; she wanted to stop, but couldn't.

"Can you hear me?"

Something seemed to snap. Kayla felt sensations coming in from all directions. *"STOP!"* she cried out in her mind.

"Shhh! Do you want to wake everyone on the ship?"

"I got that!" Kayla exclaimed out loud.

"I know," said Elan, collapsing back on the bed in exhaustion.

"Shouldn't we keep practising?"

"Not until I've had time to rest. You almost blew me to bits in there," she said, tapping her head. "You're going to have to learn a little control."

"Sorry—are you all right?" asked Kayla, concerned at how pale Elan looked.

"Yes, I'll live. But I could do with a drink; could you get me something?"

"Sure thing. I'll be back in five ticks."

Elan was left alone, looking around at the state of the room. She thought she'd only imagined things falling, but it had actually happened. No one could do that.

That night Kayla lay in bed, unable to sleep. A whole new world had opened to her. The ship seemed to be slightly translucent, with the minds of the crew like small points of light. She toyed with the idea of searching for Jaros but decided against it. Instead she played with the Stragaw piece sitting on the desk at the end of her bed. At first she just set it travelling along the board in various directions using its internal motor. Then she lifted it into the air and experimented with controlling its movement.

Satisfied that she had reasonable control, she then tried lifting up a hair clip at the same time. It took a little more effort not to drop one of the objects, but at last she got the hang of it.

Smugly satisfied with her efforts, she finally tried to get some sleep and eventually succeeded.

Commander Flynn of the Planetary Patrol was a worried man. He knew something was going on, and he didn't like it. "Betty, has Hooper from software engineering turned up yet?"

"Yes, sir. I'll send him in now."

The door slid open and a tall, thin man entered. "It's nice to meet you, commander. I understand you have some questions about our work?"

"Yes. The upgrades you've been doing on our navigation systems—can you tell me what they entailed?"

"It was just a standardization upgrade. Most ships these days use a galactic rather than solar reference system so coordinates can be used interchangeably when longer journeys are involved."

"Nothing else?"

Hooper removed the work order sheet from his briefcase and examined it for a few seconds. "Only some extraneous software upgrades; nothing else which should have had any effect. Has there been some problem, or did you want us to make some further changes?"

"No. I was just curious. Do you mind if I have a look at your order sheet?"

Hooper passed it over and Commander Flynn read it. He had not the slightest understanding of the technical jargon covering the form, but he did recognize two things — his handwriting and his signature. "Thanks for coming in, Hooper."

Hooper stood and left with a confused look on his face.

Flynn was left sitting at his desk examining the order form, still a very worried man. Opening his diary, he noted down the events and a few of his thoughts on the matter. Something would have to be done about this. As the leader of Earth's space fleet, he couldn't go around ordering things he didn't understand, let alone remember.

An idea struck him as he was closing his diary. Turning back through the pages to the date on the order form, he started reading his notes. Sure enough, there was a brief mention of the order, again in what appeared to be his handwriting.

At first there didn't seem to be anything else unusual on the page, but then he noticed something odd. The date went from 26 May to 29 May; a single leaf had been very neatly removed from the book.

Looking back through the rest of the diary, a pattern began to emerge. Roughly every twenty-five days another leaf was missing.

Sitting in her cabin, Elan heard a soft knock at the door. Much to her surprise, she found Jaros there when she opened it. "Is Kayla around?" he asked.

"No, I haven't seen her. She was gone when I woke up."

"Any idea where she could be?"

"No, sorry."

"Okay, thanks."

Jaros left and walked back down the hall, scanning the ship with his mind, hoping to pick Kayla out. He was so busy searching for her mind that he almost knocked her over when she suddenly came out of a side door.

"Ah, hello, I was just looking for you. Can we have a quick word?" asked Jaros, looking around furtively.

"If you're sure Idonea won't mind?" replied Kayla, with more sarcasm than she had intended.

"What? Oh! Come on, we can't talk here," he said, taking her by the arm and leading her down a stairwell.

Kayla pulled free. "Look, you Casanova, I'm not just one of your worshipping dolly birds you can drag off for a quick one whenever you feel like it."

Jaros looked up at her with a mixture of confusion and surprise. "Shut up for ten seconds, would you?" he said, picking her up and throwing her over his shoulder.

"Put me down now or I'll be forced to hurt you."

"Ha!" replied Jaros as they entered the main drive room.

"Don't say I didn't warn you!" said Kayla, as she started to twist and wriggle until she got her hands onto one of Jaros' legs, which she then pulled, bringing them both down on the floor.

Jaros was still lying face down on the floor too surprised to do anything, when an arm came around his neck. He felt a body leaning on his back.

"Give in?" asked Kayla.

"Give in! I haven't even started yet!" said Jaros, rolling over to grab Kayla but finding only the air in the place she had just occupied. "You're quick," he allowed.

"Thanks. You're slow," she said, jumping for him again.

"If you keep up these insults, I might withdraw my proposal," he gasped.

Kayla let go in surprise, giving Jaros just enough time to get her in a proper hold, which with his additional weight was entirely permanent.

"So, you haven't forgotten?"

"No."

"And you still mean it, even after getting your memory back?"

"Yep."

"And you really expect me to overlook the fact that you are currently engaged to someone else?"

Jaros briefly looked surprised, then rolled off her, laughing.

"What's so funny?" demanded Kayla.

"I'm not engaged to Idonea."

"So, you admit it's her!"

Jaros continued to laugh, "No, I don't admit it. It's not true."

"But Elan told me it was public knowledge."

"Yes it is. That's what's so funny."

"What do you mean?"

"Ok, I'm sorry. I'm not laughing at you, really. Well, I am, but only a little."

"You'd better explain yourself pretty quickly."

"Ok, ok, listen. Whether you like it or not, I'm in love with you. I don't exactly know why, but I am. I really can't help it; and I'm fairly sure you have the same feelings for me. If I had found out that I really was engaged to someone else when I got my memory back I would have had to break up with them, because it wouldn't be possible to feel like this about you and be with someone else. But as luck would have it, that wasn't necessary."

"Then why did Elan tell me you were engaged to Idonea if you aren't? Don't tell me she made it up, because I won't believe it."

"No, she didn't make it up, but someone did. Haven't you ever heard of tabloids? I'm royalty, and

Idonea is part of the nobility, too; and sure, we know each other. We even dance together occasionally at official events. I may not particularly like her, but it's expected."

Kayla was crouching against the wall, debating with herself about how much grovelling she was owed, which certainly seemed to be more. "I'm still cross."

"I can tell."

"Stop grinning, will you?"

"Sorry." said Jaros, doing his best to stop smiling. Then, he caught Kayla's eyes and they locked gazes for several long moments.

"And stop staring at me dreamily, too; it's not fair. I've got every right to be cross with you. You could have come to see me sooner."

"Well, I have been busy, and I didn't think you'd be reading the ship's gossip paper. It's just a thing to entertain the crew. They make stuff up for it all the time. I guess since I wasn't around no one thought to deny it, particularly since more important things were going on."

"Ok, I guess I can believe that." Kayla reached over and kissed him. "Consider yourself partially forgiven— but tell me what the heck is going on! I keep getting dribs and drabs, but I'd really like to know some answers."

"I'm afraid I don't know the whole story, either, but I probably know more than most. When Calron was first discovered by some of the early space explorers, he told them about the Gronch Empire. They set up Alceron together to eventually defend Earth. For obvious security reasons, all the humans involved on Alceron and Earth have been kept in the dark, either by withholding information or by using mind blocks. To keep a society based on ignorance together for the last thirty years has been difficult. Calron decided that the only form of government that would work would be a monarchy: hence, the title. Even so, people get restless; and we now think someone is trying to arrange a coup."

"Where do I come into all of this?"

"I don't know. Even now that the war is out in the open, no one knows any of the details of the plan. You might just be an innocent bystander who happened to be in the wrong place at the wrong time. Although, it is more likely that you are part of the plan. And, until we've figured out who's behind the coup and who is trying to have me killed, you can't afford to be associated with me. It would really be best if people got the idea we didn't like each other very much."

Kayla kicked him.

"Ouch! What was that for?"

"Just practising," Kayla replied, smiling.

Jaros pulled her close and kissed her briefly. "Remember, we can't even talk anywhere else on the ship. The anti matter drive creates enough disturbance to mess up any spy system."

"What about like this?"

"You can mind-talk?"

"Well, I just did, didn't I? What do you think I've been working on all this time?"

"And you can receive, too?"

"Yep."

"I guess so, but be careful to keep it tight so that no one else can pick it up."

"Yes, sir."

"I've got to go now before someone figures out I'm missing and starts looking for me."

The ship's comp broke in on Kayla's daydreaming. "Elan and Kayla, please report to air lock three in fifteen minutes wearing full pressure suits."

Kayla turned to Elan. "What's happening? Have we arrived?"

"No. We're scheduled to make a stop on the way, but I didn't know we would be disembarking."

"Where are we stopping?"

"I didn't think I needed to know, so I never asked. It's probably top secret so they wouldn't have told me anyway."

"Looks like we're going to find out for ourselves."

"Come on, we'd better be prompt."

The ship's storeroom had a good selection of spare suits from which Elan selected a reasonable fit for Kayla. The suits were made of a leathery dark brown material that left a lot more flexibility than Kayla had expected. Elan explained how to read the gauges and checked the fastenings before they proceeded to the air lock.

They found Jaros, Captain Breckin and Calron waiting in the airlock. Jaros raised an eyebrow as they entered.

Captain Breckin said, "What are you ladies doing here? I'm afraid this isn't a pleasure trip."

Kayla and Elan looked at each other in confusion. "We were told to report here by the ship's comp," said Kayla.

Calron broke in. "I took the liberty of inviting the young ladies. I think they may find the experience enlightening."

Breckin seemed concerned. "Are you sure that's wise?"

"They will not be in danger on a deserted moon, and a visit to my home will be necessary if they are to help us with our mission." The robot's metal chest seemed to expand slightly as it spoke; the tone of voice no longer sounded as if it required approval.

Kayla felt as if they were being discussed like a couple of children. "We are not too fragile or helpless to be allowed out, if that's what you are concerned about, Captain," said Kayla pointedly.

"Oh, very well. I suppose you aren't, at that," agreed Breckin.

"Touchdown in five seconds," announced the ship's comp. "Gravity will be point two earth normal until we depart."

Kayla waited for the crunch as they landed but was only rewarded with a feeling of falling as their acceleration dropped to that of the moon they were now on. Standing in the air lock, Kayla felt her suit inflate as the air was evacuated from the air lock. Movement was more difficult now, but still surprisingly free. Jaros made a show of checking everyone else's suits and managed to squeeze her hand surreptitiously in the process.

Kayla grinned back at him and returned the gesture, then said as crossly as she could manage, "I think you'll find everything in order. I do know how to put on a space suit, you know."

"Regulations require that everyone be checked," replied Jaros.

The outer lock opened, revealing a desolate, dimly lit reddish landscape. They emerged onto a dust-covered, cratered surface. Looking up, Kayla saw the reason for the odd colour; what appeared to be the sun was producing little more than a bright red glow.

"This is your home planet?" asked Kayla through the helmet radio.

"Yes and no," answered Calron. "This was once the moon of the planet where my creators evolved. This is where I was originally constructed."

Calron led them over the rim of a small crater.

"Kayla!" yelled Jaros, diving after her as she jumped off the rim.

Having found the inside walls too steep to negotiate easily, she had jumped out into the air, expecting to sail down majestically. Despite the low gravity, Kayla quickly picked up speed. The crunch of impact brought back all too clearly the memory of high school physics class. She suddenly remembered something about mass and inertia being independent of gravity.

Picking herself up, Kayla tried not to laugh as Jaros bounced onto the ground with even less decorum.

Calron, Breckin, and Elan arrived moments later. "If you two have finished clowning around we can continue," said Calron as he entered an opening that had appeared in the crater wall.

They entered a small cubicle, which Kayla initially took to be an air lock until the outer door had closed and she found herself floating up into the air. The others had all grasped the handrails instinctively. Kayla quickly pulled herself back down. Their suits deflated as the lift descended.

"You should find the air breathable now," announced Calron a few seconds later.

Jaros released his helmet and sniffed experimentally. He crinkled his nose a little before signalling to the others that it was okay.

The lift seemed to have been going down forever when Kayla finally felt it slowing their descent. The door slid open and they found themselves in an enormous room filled with many banks of electronic equipment. Kayla took immediate interest in their surroundings. "Is this where you were built?" she asked Calron.

"This isn't just where I was built; this was me, or at least a small part of me. There is much more."

"But why didn't they miniaturize any of it?" asked Kayla, confused.

Calron seemed a little offended. "They did the best they could. They were only a little more advanced than your race and they had a lot to fit into me."

Kayla's eye's widened with a sudden understanding of the scale of the computer system they were looking at. The comps on earth could fit into a shoebox and yet this machine with comparable miniaturization was bigger than a small office block.

"But how is it that you are now so small?"

"I'll come to that later. First, I want to show you something."

Calron took them to a small side room. It contained six chair-like structures, on which they did their best to sit while they waited. After a few moments the lights dimmed and the walls faded to invisibility.

Kayla felt herself drifting in the air above a city. On the ground she could just make out what appeared to be three-legged creatures moving around. Drawing nearer the small figures resolved into pinkish, bipedal, lizard-like creatures with long thick tails.

Jals curled his tail around his midsection for warmth while balancing unsteadily on only two feet. The Gronch had delivered another ultimatum that he had been forced to reject. War would ensue and there seemed little hope for an early victory. The Gronch technology was comparatively backward, but their mental powers more than made up for that shortcoming.

The only hope for the Jukon lay in their plan to build a mechanical telekinetic device, although every attempt so far had failed. The new computer system being developed would be able to solve the problem in a matter of minutes—or so the engineers claimed. Jals was less certain of success.

The plan was simple enough. Theory suggested that anything less complex than a human brain would be incapable of generating telekinetic energy. So, a computer system with the required ten million billion memory cells had to be constructed.

They were constructing it deep inside their largest moon in the hope that it would remain hidden from the Gronch.

Kayla felt a slight jolt as the viewpoint jumped.

Jals was furious. "But it must be possible; we've bankrupted the entire planet merely to construct you!"

"I didn't say it was impossible. I simply said that I didn't have any such ability, and I would not be able to instruct your engineers on how to build such a thing."

"But it can be done?"

"No, but your goal can be achieved." There was silence for a few seconds, then the computer added, "... eventually."

The view jumped again. This time Kayla found herself floating above the city.

Suddenly, the entire city was drenched in a blinding light. Explosions rocked the air from all directions. Kayla cringed from the noise. The scene changed again. Now she was floating over blackened crumbling structures. Small charred mounds appeared every few meters. The sky had a dim red appearance instead of the earlier bright yellowish tint. Kayla gasped. She recognized the charred remains for what they were.

The lights came back on, blinding everyone. They sat together without speaking for a few moments. Then Jaros asked, "What was the light? What happened?"

"The Gronch perfected the inertia-less drive—or more likely managed to steal it from another race. As is usual for the Gronch, they immediately thought of a nasty use for it. We had our defences arranged to protect our planet from attack.

"The inertia-less field can be generated at almost any size because it is only a means of disconnecting parts of space from each other; it doesn't require any inherent use of energy. The Gronch simply started up a field in the centre of our system and then gave our sun a gentle push towards us. Within minutes, every living thing on my planet had been pulverized. They didn't release the field until the sun was where you see it now. I survived my creators' demise partly due to the depth at which I was buried and partly because of the relative position of the moon at the time."

"Where you remained until a couple of earth explorers happened upon you a few centuries later," Jaros finished.

"Yes, and that concludes today's tour for the young ladies," said Calron. "Do you think you could escort them back to the ship now, Captain?"

"Yes, certainly. Will you two be long?"

"No, we'll be along in a minute. I just need Jaros' help to pick up a few odds and ends."

As soon as they had left Jaros turned to Calron, "What do you want me to carry?"

"Oh, nothing."

"What? But you said..."

Calron interrupted, "That was simply to get the young ladies safely back aboard the ship before anything happened."

"What's going to happen?"

"I haven't the slightest idea," Calron lied. "Humans are so unpredictable, you know."

Kayla removed her suit as soon as they were inside the ship.

"That could happen to Earth," said Elan.

"Yes, I know. Your secrecy makes more sense now. But why didn't you tell me about it?"

"Because I didn't know. That's the trouble with secrecy. You've got to just live on trust."

The ship's comp broke in, "Attention, emergency personnel report to your stations immediately! All nonessential personnel go directly to your quarters."

Breckin had already gone. Kayla and Elan were left to exchange worried looks. Elan headed for the door, but paused when Kayla didn't follow. "Come on."

"No! Jaros isn't back yet. Maybe we should go back for him."

"Don't be silly. The ship's comp will have notified him. It's probably just some sort of drill. He'll be here any second. We should be in our room, so they know where to find us in case we're needed."

Kayla would have hesitated longer, but the warning lights on the air lock started flashing to indicate it was in use.

"See? Now, come on," insisted Elan, practically dragging Kayla through the corridor and back to their room.

Breckin's finger hovered over the lever that would activate the drives and send the ship into space. He didn't like his instructions, but they were very explicit.

"Captain, we're picking up disturbances in the E-space. It could be a Gronch ship coming in."

"Keep an eye on it."

A couple of officers turned to give Breckin surprised looks, but their training prevented them from vocally questioning the wisdom of inaction. A little green light flashed on one of Breckin's displays, indicating a second entry into the air lock. He breathed a sigh of relief but continued to wait for the correct time, ignoring the increasingly worried looks from his officers. He made a mental note to commend them on their restraint at a later date.

"Sir, we're detecting multiple ships. If they are battle cruisers, they could have an operative on board."

"Let me know if anything else develops, Jenkins."

"Sir, fleet regulations state that if we suspect a superior officer may be under alien control, we must take immediate action to test our belief and then immediately remove that officer from command, should it turn out to be well-founded."

"Jenkins, during an emergency the normal social requirements for privacy are waived. In future, make a mental scan immediately. Then apologize when time permits."

Jenkins turned a little red at the reprimand and quickly checked the captain's mind.

"And what about the rest of you? At least Jenkins here remembered regulations."

Kayla couldn't sit down. She paced back and forth in the small room. "What's happening?" she asked, looking towards the comp console.

"It won't answer. During an emergency, secrecy regulations come into effect. The ship's comp won't tell anyone anything more than they actually need to know. Any alien telepath would have to search through every mind on the ship in order to discover what we're doing."

"Bother!" complained Kayla. "Does this sort of attack happen often?" Elan didn't reply. She was staring open-mouthed at the dice Kayla was fiddling with in mid-air. "What's wrong?"

"That's you?"

"It calms my nerves; shouldn't I be doing it?"

"No, it's fine. It's just that you shouldn't be able to."

"Why? Because I'm from Earth?"

"No, because no one can. The controls in the game pieces are ultra-sensitive, but I've never seen anyone lift more than a feather under normal gravity."

Kayla started to say something about her experiments with the bed, but then thought better of it. Suddenly, she grabbed her head and screamed, "Arrghh!"

"What's wrong?"

Kayla stumbled onto the bed and curled up in pain.

"Block your mind, like we practised before," said Elan, realizing what was happening. "Build a wall around yourself."

The bed and desk started to shake.

At exactly the predetermined time, Breckin threw the lever down, instantly shooting the ship on its way out of the system. Breckin brushed the sweat from his brow, safe in the knowledge they couldn't be attacked at ultra light speed.

"Make a heading for Alceron," he instructed.

"But, sir, we could be followed. Shouldn't we go somewhere else first?"

Breckin had voiced a similar complaint, but wasn't going to admit that to his subordinates. He fixed the young officer with a stony look and replied, "Maybe I want them to follow us!"

Kayla was still curled up on her bed. Elan had been trying to get her attention, now that she seemed to have relaxed.

"Are you okay?" Elan asked.

"Yes, it's stopped. Once I did what you said, it was all right."

"It must have been a Gronch attack."

Kayla's eye's widened, "Something's wrong!"

"Is it attacking you again?"

"No, not that, something's gone," she said, her mind searching. "JAROS!"

Elan quickly started to feel through the ship. It only took a few seconds because Jaros was usually so clear. "You're right! We'll have to go back for him."

"Comp, switch me through to the captain."

"He's on the bridge. Is this important?"

"Yes, now switch me through," insisted Elan.

Breckin's voice boomed out of the wall, "What is it?" He didn't seem to be in a very good mood.

"Elan here, sir, we think the prince is missing."

The speaker remained silent for a few seconds before they heard the captain reply, "Bother!"

"How long before we can get back to pick him up?" Elan wanted to know.

"We won't be going back. We are continuing to Alceron. Thanks for letting me know, though."

The speaker went dead, leaving Kayla and Elan staring at each other.

Breckin cursed under his breath. Now the instructions about not turning back no matter what began to make sense. He sat pondering the true meaning of a little green light on his console.

Commander Flynn was a nervous wreck. The alien attack had left Earth in turmoil, which put the planetary patrol's already fragile political situation on very thin ice. He was asked to explain their failure to defend Earth, identify the attackers or initiate a counter-blow after having spent so much money on an otherwise useless space fleet.

He tried to point out to the politicians that it had been a surprise attack by an advanced race of aliens. To top it all off, today was the twenty-first of June, which meant that someone would remove today's diary entry. To relax, he slid open his top drawer, took out a small bottle of aspirin, removed one and swallowed it. Turning to his diary, he noted: Took aspirin at 9:20 to calm nerves.

Suddenly, awareness hit him, he stared at what he had written, and then examined the bottle more closely.

It didn't have a label. Why did he think it contained aspirin? He quickly noted: Bottle is not labelled as aspirin. Why did I think it was aspirin?

Panic set in. What could he do if it was poison? He hit the vidphone switch. "Get me a doctor quickly! This is an emergency."

Endless seconds ticked by while he was switched through to a local hospital. He argued with a receptionist before she eventually agreed to page a doctor. Finally, the face of a man wearing a white coat appeared on the screen.

"Hello, I'm Doctor Ferdon. What do you want?"

"I've just taken ... " began Flynn, when a puzzled expression suddenly stole over his face. He shook his head a couple of times and then began to relax. "I'm terribly sorry. I seem to have been connected to the wrong extension," he said, quickly pressing the disconnect switch.

Removing a small knife from his drawer, Flynn carefully cut out the page from his diary.

CHAPTER TEN

"Guess what?" asked Elan. "We've been invited to the VIP lounge to view the docking."

"When's that?"

"In about two hours…Cheer up. He'll be okay."

"What do you mean?"

"Jaros. He always comes through in one piece."

Kayla realized she must have been a bit of a drag to live with these last few days. "Sorry. I'm all right, really."

"Good."

Kayla had an idea. "How about you? You haven't mentioned a boyfriend. I know a bloke back home you might like."

"An Earth guy? I don't think so!"

"Prejudice rears its ugly head?"

"No. I don't have anything against Earthlings. I just wouldn't want to go out with one," said Elan, realizing as the words came out that she'd put herself right in it. "Okay, I admit it, but it's all a bit academic now that the nearest one is over thirty light-years away."

"True enough; still, I think you'd really suit each other."

That evening Kayla and Elan entered the VIP lounge. They were late, with only a few minutes left before docking. Most of the other VIPs were already there, feigning boredom at the image of the spaceport that *Destiny* was approaching. The spaceport loomed into view like a mural resolving on the lounge's vid screen.

"Hello," said Idonea. "Kayla and Elan, isn't it? How nice to see you again. This must be quite a treat for you."

Fortunately, the ship's comp interrupted before Kayla had a chance to reply. "Please secure your belongings and hold onto a stabilizer rail. During docking the ship will be under variable acceleration for a few minutes. Thirty seconds to docking manoeuvres."

Together Elan and Kayla moved over to one of the handholds scattered around the walls. The base already covered a large section of the vid screen, but nothing betrayed its actual scale.

As they neared, Kayla could see the space station rotating very slowly. She thought the rotation too slow to generate reasonable acceleration. She soon realized her error when a small dot detached itself from the structure and slowly resolved into a ship before disappearing off the edge of the screen. Her stomach lurched unpleasantly as *Destiny* dropped into free fall, beginning a gut-wrenching series of manoeuvres to bring them into the docking port of the space station.

Kayla was having a lot of trouble keeping a dignified hold on the stabilizer. Idonea was looking at her disparagingly and MT'd loudly to the other VIPs, *"I do hope the earthling isn't sick."*

The ship's comp chimed in. "Docking will be completed in five seconds."

Kayla counted to herself: five, four, three, two, and then pushed Idonea's legs gently a split second before the ship's magnetic grapples locked onto the spinning planetoid, returning normal gravity to the ship. Idonea sprawling across the floor.

Kayla managed to keep a straight face as she politely offered a helping hand, which Idonea, struggling to her feet, pretended not to see.

Kayla felt a bit guilty. She decided to be a little more forgiving in the future. She turned to Elan and changed the subject. "I didn't see the planet Alceron as we approached. Is it behind us or eclipsed by the base?" asked Kayla.

"What planet?"

"THE planet."

Once she figured out what Kayla was going on about, Elan explained, "No, we don't live on a planet. This system doesn't have any worth settling on; anyway, building in space is easier. There are seven of these bases. Together they make up Alceron. That's also how we remain hidden. The Gronch survey teams usually only check out planets. In this system none of them are habitable, so we stand a good chance of being overlooked. Come on, Kayla. The locks will be open in a few minutes," urged Elan.

Elan rushed Kayla back to their room, where Elan packed a shoulder bag in less than a minute. "What's the hurry?" Kayla asked.

"If we get there quickly we won't have to queue, and I want you to meet my family," replied Elan. She glanced around the room one more time before grabbing Kayla by the hand and dragging her back out into the passageway.

"You won't mention anything about…?" asked Kayla, nervously pointing at her head.

"No. I told you I wouldn't tell anyone."

"Thanks. It's just until I get a better hang of it."

"Yep, I know. As if you didn't have it already!"

"What do your parents do?" asked Kayla, changing the subject.

Elan paused in mid-stride, her face showing nothing of the internal turmoil she was feeling. "I don't have any parents."

"I'm sorry. I didn't know."

"It's not just me; lots of us don't. To get a whole generation of telepaths, there was a certain amount of baby snatching. Not from normal families. Just from orphanages. They also did a little family planning by picking up latent telepaths, removing a few eggs or sperm and paying for surrogate mothers."

"Isn't that a little amoral?"

"No," said Elan, surprised. "No one was hurt. We used mind blocks so apart from a few who underwent hypnosis, most people didn't even know they had been snatched. How else could you make certain that the right people had children together? It certainly wouldn't be very nice to kidnap people and bring them to Alceron, only to find out they didn't want to live here."

A fact clicked in Kayla's mind. "So you people were behind all those UFO sightings and abduction rumours?"

"Well, some of them, maybe. Anyway, as I was saying, a lot of us didn't have real parents. They tried to set up pseudo-families with mother and father figures, but mostly it didn't work."

"Why not?"

"No one knows. It may have been the telepathy. The pseudo-parents weren't telepathic, so they sort of lost touch. The kids in each family just started looking after each other, and since the psychologists couldn't think of any better system, they eventually just left us to it."

"So when you said family, you meant your adopted brothers and sisters?"

"Yes, but using the word adopted could get you in trouble."

"Consider it withdrawn."

Elan waved her arm around vaguely at their entire surroundings. "What do you think?" she asked.

"Of what?"

"Alceron!"

Kayla re-examined the passage they were walking through. "I hadn't realized we'd left the ship."

Elan looked offended, "Is that all you can say? You didn't notice the wide passages, the fresh air," Elan took a deep breath, "and the subdued but pleasant lighting? All the comforts of home!"

"Oh! It looks very nice."

Elan realized Kayla was humouring her. "I'll show you the sights later. Then you'll be impressed."

The passage they were following opened onto a wide walkway bustling with people. It appeared to be a shopping centre of some kind, but Elan wouldn't let Kayla stop to look around. They turned down a passageway. The signpost indicated the way to the stationary train.

"Why is it called a stationary train?" asked Kayla.

"That's just a local joke. The planetoid is in the shape of a sphere. The train runs around the circumference but in the opposite direction to the planetoid's rotation, so the train is stationary relative to the sphere when you get on, but it becomes truly stationary when it's moving because it runs at the same speed as the sphere rotates."

"Why didn't they make it go in the other direction?"

"Because then everyone would weigh twice as much. This way you simply become weightless as the train picks up speed."

"Oh, I see. Couldn't we walk?" suggested Kayla hopefully.

"No, it's miles away. Come on, it's fun," said Elan, as a small bullet-like train pulled up. "There aren't many people on at this time of day so we can have some fun."

"Oh, goody," lied Kayla. She sat down in one of the seats and took a good grip on the railing. "You can play. I'm not moving until we get there."

The doors slid shut and the train began to accelerate. Kayla could feel the sensation of falling build immediately. Soon she was having trouble keeping in the seat. Elan floated around overhead, encouraging her to let go.

After a couple of minutes a warning bell sounded and Elan quickly pulled herself down next to Kayla. The train slowed and stopped.

"This is our stop," said Elan. She led Kayla off the train. "Unless you want to go around once and get off next time."

Kayla ignored her remark.

A few minutes later they arrived at a door. It slid open and the comp said, "Welcome home, Elan."

"It's good to be home."

The two women stepped into an expansive living area. To the right were an array of sofas and a small table. On the left there appeared to be a kitchen unit. Another door stood in the wall opposite from the one through which they had just arrived.

A young lad of about sixteen slouched across one of the couches. He had long hair and wore a pair of jeans and an old shirt, both of which had seen better days. He looked up lazily. "Hi sis. What's for dinner?"

"You will be if you can't pretend to be civilized."

"I only asked, and it is your turn."

"I've been away for a month and all you're worried about is your stomach?"

"I'm a growing lad. Aren't you going to introduce your friend?"

"This is Kayla. She's from Earth," said Elan. "This is my youngest brother, Rastus. He's not yet fully housebroken, but we're working on it."

"Hi," said Kayla.

"Hi," replied Rastus, not one to waste words. *"Not bad,"* thought Rastus to his sister, trying to look cool.

"She's too old for you, dreamer. Anyway she's only got eyes for Jaros. And don't be so certain that she can't pick up on your tight-beam thoughts."

Rastus's eyes glanced deeply into Kayla's, trying to catch some hint that she had heard, but her eyes betrayed nothing and her mind block deflected his probe without even revealing its presence.

"You are making fun of me. She's an Earth girl!"

"If you say so, little brother."

"Now, go and get the others, will you?" she continued aloud.

"Yes, oh great and wise one!" said Rastus jumping out of his seat and bowing up and down until Elan took a swipe at him.

"Have a seat. Would you like a drink?" asked Elan, moving into the kitchen area and setting out a line of mugs.

"Yes, thanks. I'll stand for a minute. It's nice to be in a decent-sized room after being cooped up in the ship."

While Elan was looking for something in the cupboard, a large sandy-haired young man stepped silently into the room. When he saw Kayla, he held a single finger up to his lips and winked, and then stalked silently up behind Elan in the kitchen, grabbed her around the middle and flipped her upside down.

"Ahh, Kayla, meet Silas," said Elan, her head dangling a few inches off the floor.

"Nice to meet you," he said, extending a hand to shake, belatedly remembering to flip Elan the right way up.

"Charmed, I'm sure," replied Kayla.

Suddenly, the room had become crowded; Rastus returned with two more siblings: a girl with long dark hair about the same age as Rastus, and the other, a young man with short dark hair.

Elan and Silas were talking in whispers over the coffee and seemed to have forgotten her, so Kayla introduced herself.

"Hi, I'm Kayla. I'm from Earth."

The dark-haired young man took charge. "I'm Caius, Elan's only normal brother, and this is Nessa." He turned to Elan and Silas and said, "We'll be in the lounge. Bring the drinks through, will you?" before ducking the spoon that came flying in his general direction. "Come and give me a hug, you rat!" Elan shouted after him.

He turned to Kayla, "Excuse me a minute, won't you, while I teach my sister how to behave in front of guests?"

Nessa whispered in her ear, "He's not really normal. It's just a front he puts up whenever we have company."

A short while later, Elan found herself on the couch next to Kayla. Nessa quietly handed out the hot drinks before sitting down on the floor in front of Silas.

Caius said, "So sis, tell us about your travels to parts foreign," Everyone leaned forward expectantly.

Elan proceeded to relate a colourful, if not entirely accurate, account of their adventures to date, leaving out only a few little details here and there.

When Elan had finished, the four others persistently harassed Kayla until she agreed to tell the story of her escape from the Gronch back on Earth. She did her best, editing it in a similar way as did Elan, emphasizing some of the action and removing a few personal events.

When she was finished Caius said, "I think that explains it."

"But what are we going to do about it? The whole thing smells to me," added Silas.

"What are you two talking about?"

They exchanged looks and then Caius answered, "There was an announcement about an hour ago, just before you arrived. They said that the prince was missing, presumed dead, and that Ranic would be taking command until further notice."

"But he isn't dead," said Elan. "There's a good chance he's still on that moon."

"Come on Elan, a Gronch battle cruiser with operators on board is hardly likely to miss the only sentient mind in an entire system; and the Gronch don't take prisoners."

Kayla interrupted, "He's not dead."

Caius tried to remove his foot from his mouth. "Sorry. I guess it is possible they weren't picked up."

"I didn't say I thought he wasn't dead. I said he isn't. I'd know."

"What do you mean?" asked Elan.

"I don't know what I mean. All I know is that if he were dead I'd know, so at the moment he's still alive. The same way I knew when he wasn't on the ship, I guess."

Caius broke in, "I thought you had no MT?"

"I never said either way."

"But even if you have, you can't sense him from this distance. Not unless—" He stopped in mid-sentence.

"Unless what?" asked Kayla.

"Oh, nothing," replied Caius weakly.

Silas said, "You're getting off the point anyway. The fact is, Ranic is using this as an excuse to take control. With the Gronch war out in the open there's no longer any legitimate excuse for the secrecy act to continue; but you can lay odds he'll find a reason to continue it, which prevents anyone from questioning his authority."

"I never liked the system when Jaros and his father were in control, but I certainly don't plan to be ordered around by the likes of Ranic without knowing what's going on," agreed Caius.

"Ssh," said Elan. "What if the city comp is listening?"

Rastus smiled knowingly. "Don't worry about that. I made a few minor modifications to our console."

Elan looked at him warmly. "See, and you thought I was just being mean sending you to all those extra classes."

"You were just being mean, but I forgive you anyway."

A deep ringing sound erupted from the room speakers and the console sprung to life, "Attention please! This is an official announcement. We expect a Gronch attack in the next few days. The current highest rating operative is Idonea Karvelas. She will be controlling the Alceron fleet. Announcement ends."

After a few moments Rastus broke the silence, "She can't handle the fleet! She only wins at Stragaw because she can use more pieces than anyone else. She will cause the massacre of half our ships in the first five minutes."

Silas, Elan, and Caius exchanged worried glances. They each knew, as qualified pilots, any or even all of them could be called into the battle.

"That does it," said Caius. "If it was Jaros, it would be different."

Another deep ringing alarm came from the speakers, "Attention please! This is an official announcement. Graeme Masters has lodged a challenge. A game has been scheduled for twenty hundred hours. Announcement ends."

"That's the third time today that idiotic thing has lit up," said Nessa. "If it does it again, I'm going to kick it."

"Wasn't Graeme that bloke on the ship?" asked Kayla.

"Yes," replied Elan. "But he can't control enough ships. Not by himself. It's a pity."

"Why doesn't he handle the strategy and simply give his instructions to a good operative?"

"In theory he could; there are no rules against it, but there's never been a pair that could communicate well enough to actually play better that way than alone.

Elan suddenly sprung to life. "Kayla can do it! She can control lots of ships."

"Really?" asked Silas and Caius in harmony.

"No. I've never even played the game. I wouldn't know what to do."

"That wouldn't matter. Graeme would tell you what to do. You'd just be acting as a relay station. Easy, really."

"Sure," said Kayla, feeling very doubtful.

Caius still seemed worried. "Do we really have to fight the Gronch? Maybe they're not as rotten as we've been led to believe."

"The ones that came after Jaros and me didn't seem too friendly," said Kayla.

"But how do you know they didn't just want to say hello? Did you try talking to them?"

"Of course not! You don't talk with a giant green monster."

"I guess not."

Silas said, "The point is that we are going to be asked to die while valiantly attacking a Gronch battle cruiser. Now I, for one, never signed on for that kind of duty. I'm rather fond of life and would like to explore the alternatives, before jumping out of the trench with a shout of `Tally Ho!' and charging like a maniac toward the enemy."

Caius interrupted, "I think we should clear up a little matter regarding Kayla before this conversation goes any further."

"What do you mean?" asked Elan.

"If we are going to discuss the security of members of this family, then non–family members shouldn't be present."

"Don't be so rude, Caius, she's my guest; she stays as long as I want her to."

Kayla felt awkward and said, "It's okay. I can disappear while you talk."

"I wasn't actually suggesting you go anywhere. There is another option."

Kayla caught a glimmer of thoughts flying around the room and decided she was being looked at rather too intensely by five pairs of eyes. They seemed to be at a bit of a loss as to who should speak. Finally, Silas said, "It's clear you've become a close friend of Elan's and you are a long way from home. It's very possible you may never see Earth again. We would like to know if you would consider joining us."

Kayla was speechless; she'd never had any family other than Mark and Alfred. "I don't know what to say," she finally said.

"Yes is one option," suggested Nessa helpfully.

"But you hardly know me!"

"We've seen enough," said Rastus.

"I don't know."

"I think she's trying to back out of it," said Silas.

Elan joined in, "Yes, she's looking decidedly skittish, this calls for plan B."

"What's plan B."

Five voices chanted, "Three, two, one ... tickle," and jumped her.

"Stop!" cried Kayla between breaths while trying to fight them off.

"Not until you say yes."

"Okay, okay, I say yes."

They stopped reluctantly, "Awh gee whiz," said Rastus. "Girls give in too easily."

"We should link," said Caius.

"Not until everyone has had time to think about the problem separately," said Elan.

"Good idea, and you two probably want a chance to unpack and relax. We'll reconvene in two hours," said Caius.

"I'll show you the rest of the house," said Nessa.

CHAPTER ELEVEN

*K*ayla leaned back, luxuriating in a real bubble bath. The feeling of warmth all around her, both physically and mentally. She opened her mind to take it in completely. Five glowing minds were close by, each different but all friendly. She looked further. The whole massive planetoid was glowing with little points of light — thousands of them.

She felt like she could fly anywhere. As she spread herself thinner out into space, she sensed the other planetoids; each one packed with tens of thousands of minds.

Kayla suddenly thought of Mark. She might never see him again. Suddenly she felt rather selfish, enjoying herself when Mark was probably worried sick about her. He might have been hurt in the Gronch attack. She wanted to search toward Earth, but she didn't know which way to go.

"Elan?"

"Hang on a sec, I'm just on the vid phone."

"Sorry."

"No, don't worry, I'm free now. I was just catching up on a few messages. What did you want?"

"Which way's Earth?"

"Huh?"

"I want to try to contact Mark, but I don't know which way to go."

"You can't..." started Elan, and then thought better of it. *"Just concentrate on him, try to remember how his mind felt."*

"I don't know how his mind felt. I wasn't telepathic the last time I saw him."

"Of course you were, you just didn't know it then. Think about it."

"Okay, I'll try it."

Mark stood rigidly to attention. The sergeant, a burly man in his early thirties, was glowering at him and one of his classmates, Alex.

"What do you call this?" the sergeant shouted, pointing at the open panel and disassembled drive system.

"We were just interested in seeing how it worked, sir," volunteered Alex bravely.

The sergeant turned a brighter shade of red and shouted, "And what was the first thing you were told when you started training on these ships?"

"Not to touch the drive system?" suggested Mark.

"And do you think ripping it into tiny little pieces qualifies as touching it?"

They both remained silent.

"By God, when I was a trainee, I didn't disregard rules left, right and centre. We were taught to respect authority and to follow orders."

"Ahh, but you had a different sergeant," said Alex, and immediately wished he hadn't.

For a few horrible seconds they thought the sergeant might actually explode; then he seemed to calm down a fraction and his expression slowly turned into a wicked grin. It was evident that he had thought of a just and fitting punishment. Mark and Alex held their breath.

The sergeant spoke quietly. "The commander has asked for two volunteers for a special assignment. Do I hear any takers?"

Mark started to ask what the assignment would involve, but then realized it wasn't relevant. "We'd both like to volunteer, sir."

"We would?" asked Alex, surprised.

Mark kicked him. "Ouch! Oh! Yes we would."

Later that day they were trying to put the assignment out of their minds. Mark lifted his glass and polished off the remaining lemonade. It was hard, he realized, to look cool while drinking lemonade, but since the taste of anything stronger made him queasy, he simply had to try drinking it in a masterful fashion.

Alex was pointing toward some girls. "Check out those girls. I think they've been looking our way."

"They're a bit young, you know. Can't you tell their age?"

"Sure I can, but I like younger women. Anyway, when I'm 70 and she's 65 it won't matter much, will it?"

"Until you find out they have to be home by 11:30."

"Yeah, that can be a problem. How about her? And look, she's got a friend for you."

"And look, they've both brought their old boyfriends. I bet they'll be friendly too."

"Oh."

Mark toyed with his empty glass. He was glad to get an evening's leave before the assignment but was a little worried by the way everyone was treating them like condemned men. He ordered another drink. The problem with lemonade was that drowning your sorrows in it just didn't work the way it was supposed to. Finding Kayla gone and the house destroyed had been a nasty shock.

At first they tried to tell him that she'd been killed, but he hadn't believed it. And eventually, someone came forward who claimed to have seen a man and a woman running from the house a few minutes before it exploded. It had to have been Kayla and Jaros. The question remained: where was she now? If she had access to a console, then she would have found a way to contact him. He took another gulp of lemonade. It didn't help. Alex seemed to have hooked onto another likely prospect.

Mark spilled his lemonade when Alex stumbled into him. Looking up to see what had made Alex fall he found that a goodly number of angry people were looking at them and slowly closing in.

"Arrghh umph," said Mark as he landed with a thud on the ground a short distance from Alex.

Alex said, "I was thinking of leaving soon anyway. It wasn't much of a joint."

"What the heck did you do in there?" asked Mark.

"Nothing!"

"Sure, we just got chucked out because you did nothing!"

"I just used my sure-fire-gets-them-every-time-girls-can't-resist-it line."

"Not the one about trumpet players? I've told you before that someone might take offence, and no one would believe it anyway."

"No, not that one. I just told them we were both patrol pilots."

"And?"

"And they got nasty. It seems that since the attack on Earth, we're no longer quite the heroes we used to be."

They walked slowly back towards the base. Mark was nursing his left leg slightly, and Alex spent a good deal of time prodding his darkening right eye and muttering to himself. When they had passed beyond the bright city lights, Alex stopped and stared up at the sky.

Mark asked, "What are you looking at? Did you see something?"

"No. I was just wondering which one they came from."

"That one," said Mark, confidently pointing toward a star.

"How do you know?"

"I don't; I just picked that one at random. Does it really make any difference?"

Alex thought for a minute, "I guess not."

"Mark?"

Mark spun around looking for the voice.

"What's wrong?" asked Alex.

"Nothing—I just thought I heard someone call my name."

Alex looked worried. Mark hadn't been himself ever since the fire. "She'll turn up."

"Mark, can you hear me?"

"Yes," said Mark.

"That's the spirit," said Alex.

"What?" asked Mark.

"Talk with your mind. I can't hear you."

"How am I supposed to do that?"

"Do what?"

"Ssh—I'm trying to talk to Kayla."

"Sorry," said Alex as a puzzled look came over his face.

"Remember that bully at school, the one who roughed you up whenever he caught you alone, until I started turning up? Try calling out to me like you used to then."

Mark concentrated hard, but nothing happened, then he had an idea. "Alex, will you throw me on the ground."

"Huh?"

"Just do it, okay?"

"Sure, why not?" Alex put his right leg behind Mark, grabbed his shoulder and pulled him around and down, pulling back a little to soften the impact. Mark hit the wet grass and sure enough, the memories came back. *"Kayla!"*

"I heard that! Do it again! Try to say something else!"

Alex watched Mark sitting on the wet grass with a funny expression on his face.

"Where the hell are you?"

"You've got it!"

"Why haven't you called me?"

"That's really good."

"And why did you blow the house up?"

"It's great to hear your voice — well sense it, anyway. I thought I'd never see you again."

"Will you stop babbling and tell me what's going on?"

"Sorry. Hang on a sec, while I get out of the bath."

"What?"

"Are you okay?" asked Alex.

"I'm fine; we're just waiting for Kayla to get out of the bath."

Alex stood with his arms out straight and looked to the far right.

"What are you doing?" Mark asked.

Alex looked at Mark as if he was stupid. "I thought it would be obvious, since it's your delusion. I'm offering her a towel and looking the other way. I was brought up to be a gentleman."

Mark grinned, and signalled Alex to be quiet. "Ssh, she's back."

"This will take a while. I'll start from the night we were attacked by the aliens..."

Alex stood by as Mark sat down, apparently listening to something only he could hear. A good hour or so passed before he finally came back to the world of the living and started filling Alex in on what he'd learned.

CHAPTER TWELVE

"Come on, Kayla, you can try to find Jaros after the meeting," insisted Elan, dragging her into the lounge.

Everyone turned to Rastus. He seemed a little embarrassed. "I think it would be better if Caius chaired the meeting. I know it's my turn, but this is serious."

"Are you sure?" asked Caius.

Rastus nodded.

"Okay," said Caius, "The meeting is open. The subject up for discussion is the security of the members of our family; most specifically, the qualified pilots, and secondly, the security of Alceron in as much as it will affect the safety of the family, and of course, that of our friends and acquaintances. Suggestions are invited."

Kayla spoke up. "Caius, I'd like to add something to what you just said."

"Go ahead."

"Well, this may not be relevant, but there are two other people in my life, Jaros and Mark. I won't agree with any decision that would put them in danger. And secondly, I think we should consider the lives of everyone else on Earth and Alceron, and possibly other alien races as well."

"Hear, hear!" said Elan.

"Ssh, Elan, this isn't a debate. We are just trying to get some guidelines set up for discussion." Caius turned to Kayla. "I didn't mean to sound like we didn't care for the rest of humanity. Accepting Kayla's amendments to the agenda, does anyone have anything that they would like to say?"

Silas said, "I've been considering the obvious option; namely, that we steal a space cruiser and set off for an uncharted system where we settle down and live happily ever after."

"We can't run out on everyone!" said Elan.

"If you'll let me finish," continued Silas. "There are several problems with this option. First, finding a habitable system may be difficult. If the Gronch race has existed for as long as we think, then there are probably very few habitable systems that aren't occupied. There would be obvious dangers in searching for one. Second, assuming for a moment that we did find one, it would then be necessary to live completely off our own resources, and that could prove difficult for such a small group. Third, the Gronch threat would continue; at some point in the future, when we had populated the system, a Gronch cruiser could turn up and wipe out the lot of us, or our descendants."

"So you're saying that the best defence, running away, is not open to us."

Silas nodded. "Basically, yes."

"What about the idea of Kayla teaming up with someone like Graeme?" asked Rastus.

"It's no good," said Nessa. "I checked the rules. Teams aren't allowed."

"But that's silly; the game rules shouldn't apply when we're in a real battle," said Rastus.

"No; remember that the game is only an approximation of battle conditions," explained Caius. "All the rules are designed to make it as close to the real thing as possible. So if there is a rule about teams, then that means a team would run into problems during a real battle."

"We could hide until after the battle and just ignore any call up orders," suggested Nessa.

"Any problems with that?" prompted Caius.

"We may be arrested after the battle. But that's better than being dead," said Silas.

"And if our side loses, then we could end up dead anyway."

"So unless we come up with a way of significantly increasing our side's chances of winning we should use that plan."

"What about Calron?" put in Kayla.

"What about him?"

"Well, he seemed to know what was going on. I got the impression he had a plan. Maybe we should talk to him."

"True enough. Do you think he'd talk to you if you could get to him?"

"I don't know. Maybe."

"Okay, any other ideas?" asked Caius.

The room remained silent.

"In that case, I suggest we link."

They all moved forward and linked hands. Kayla followed suit, wondering what was to come.

Elan said, "It's real easy Kayla, just relax. We'll do the rest."

"Okay, I'm game." She closed her eyes and waited.

"Let down your block, dummy; we can't get through a brick wall," complained Elan.

"Oops, sorry."

"That's better..."

When the contact broke, Kayla found herself completely alone again — even though they were still together in the room.

"Right," said Caius. "Is everyone clear about what their part is?"

Everyone nodded.

"Good, then let's get on with it."

"Did I do okay, Elan?"
"You did fine."

Nessa was wearing a minidress. It was the sort of dress that could have gotten a girl arrested in a conventionally moral society; fortunately for Nessa there were very few of those left, and Alceron wasn't one of them. She didn't look sixteen any longer; nor did she look innocent.

The stores officer practically choked on his drink. "Can I help you?" he stuttered.

She flashed her dazzling smile at him, leaving the poor officer completely speechless. "Yes, I do hope so. I know it sounds silly, but I'm lost. I grew up on one of the mining ships so I don't really know my way around here."

"Certainly; where are you trying to go?"

"The Balteron room."

"Yes, I know that place. Are they holding a party there?"

"Yes. It's a twenty-first. I've never been to one before—do you think this dress is suitable?" said Nessa, giving a quick twirl, elevating her already skimpy dress to new heights.

"Very suitable," he managed to say. "Perhaps I should show you the way."

"Oh! Would you?"

"It will only take a minute."

Silas and Caius watched them disappear down the corridor. "Come on, Silas. She can take care of herself."

Silas reluctantly followed Caius into the storeroom. They quickly found the objects they were looking for and retreated.

"We're out, Nessa. You can ditch him."

"No sooner said than done," replied Nessa.

"Close your eyes," Nessa said to the store's officer.

"Why?"

"Just do it!" she insisted.

"Okay." He closed his eyes and felt the electric shock of an unexpected kiss. He waited hopefully for a moment before opening his eyes, only to find the passageway empty. He headed back to the storeroom, a little confused, but still wearing some smudged lipstick and a silly grin.

Six levels above the storeroom, the loading bay bustled with activity. All of the small attack ships were being readied for takeoff. Kayla walked alongside Rastus, Silas, and Caius. The robot rolled along behind them. They all wore the white coveralls of safety inspectors. Kayla was trying to look confident and self-assured, but she was scared. She wasn't so certain it was the right thing to do anymore.

Caius picked one of the air locks that appeared to be vacant and they all crowded in. Seconds later they were inside a ship, which also proved to be empty. Rastus set to work on the console. It was critical that the central comp didn't discover them too soon.

Now they had little else to do but wait. No one seemed very keen on talking; in fact, they seemed to be looking at her strangely, their eyes glassy and emotionless. Kayla found herself shaking with nerves and trying to resist the urge to escape. Time ticked away slowly until the robot started threatening them.

"I am aware that you have kidnapped me and the authorities will catch up with you soon. Kidnapping me has placed Alceron in serious danger. You should return me immediately."

"Can't you shut Calron up, Rastus?"

"No, not without killing it."

"Pity."

The warning siren started.

Silas leapt to his feet. "That's it; they must be preparing to attack us." He grabbed Kayla roughly and held her while Caius started to tie her up.

Silas looked a little guilty and tried to apologize. "Sorry about this, Kayla, but we all agreed it was better to sacrifice you than for all of us to die."

The robot tried to make a run for the air lock, but he wasn't built for speed. Rastus had him before he could get there.

Caius took the pilot's seat. "Is everyone strapped down?"

Kayla felt the lurch as they disconnected from the planetoid. They drifted for a few seconds before Caius activated the main engines, which restored some feeling of gravity.

Gontor felt an irritating tickling at the edge of his mind. At first he just ignored it, but then he realized it was coming from one of the primitives' spacecraft. He felt a little sick at the thought of being touched by such a backward mind, as if it might rub off on him.

They are probably going to plead for mercy, he thought. Oh well, it should be fun toying with them a little before killing them.

"Oh great and masterful Gronch captain."

Gontor raised his left eye slightly. Perhaps they weren't quite as backward as he had thought.

"We know that we can never hope to defeat your powerful vessel, so we have come to offer you the things you seek."

"And what do you think I seek, little creature?"

"Two things: first, the alien computer that has been plotting against your great and peaceful race, and second, our most powerful MT operative. In exchange, we ask only that you leave us in peace."

Gontor raised his other eye. This was an unexpected development. Could these creatures really be that stupid. Gontor laughed at himself — of course they could! After all, according to the scientists, these creatures evolved from something that lived in trees, which helped to explain why they were so long and gangly.

But Gontor wasn't stupid, *"Open your minds. If you are lying, you will die."* He examined each of the minds on the little ship. They all seemed rather distressed at the thought of giving over the female creature. But there was no hint of any ulterior motive.

The female's mind was blocked and try as he might he couldn't break down the wall around it. Perhaps it was the distance. That would explain it. She couldn't be as strong as that, not such a flimsy little creature.

"Very well, I accept your offer. Bring your ship in. It won't be attacked."

"Thank you, oh great and mighty warrior."

"This will never work. You can't trust the Gronch," said Rastus.

"We all agreed, even Kayla, that this was the best way: the most good for the most people, the lesser of two evils. None of us like it, but it's got to be done." Caius appeared to be trying to justify it to himself as much as to Rastus.

They were interrupted by the clank of the ship's air locks connecting. Rastus and Silas reluctantly first carried the robot and then Kayla into the interconnecting air lock and closed the door.

The moment the door closed, Kayla pulled open a panel on the side of the robot and extracted a portable space suit. She fumbled with it desperately, hindered by the weightlessness, knowing that she only had a few seconds before the Gronch air lock would open.

The door began to slide open as she finished fastening the plastic helmet. She pushed the robot as hard as she could towards the door and waited for a second to see it sail into the Gronch ship. Then grabbing hold of the air lock door, she mentally scanned the Alceronian ship with her mind, until she found the main control lever and pushed it forward.

As the robot sailed into the Gronch ship it had some very surprising thoughts. Suddenly, it wanted to be very near the Gronch captain; in fact the idea of a really good hug seemed strangely inviting. In the weightless conditions of a ship-to-ship linkup it found manoeuvring a simple matter of Newtonian mechanics. Within seconds it had slipped passed the Gronch guards and up a passageway. Moments later it sailed happily into the bridge and wrapped its little metal arms around the Gronch captain. "Kiss me quickly," it said blissfully.

Caius, Silas and Rastus, who had just recovered from the unexpected acceleration, watched with surprise as the view screen showed the gigantic battle cruiser exploding in a dazzling display of fireworks. They were even more surprised when the air lock opened and Kayla stepped back into the ship.

Rastus managed to enunciate their feelings. "What in heaven's name is going on?"

Kayla smiled broadly, "It worked, just as you said it would. Here, take these." She handed out the little green pills and waited for their memory blocks to dissolve.

"It seems a pity for even a normal comp to die," said Rastus. "But at least I programmed it to experience true love for just a few moments before the detonation."

"Very thoughtful of you," said Silas.

"I still think I should have been allowed to come too," complained Elan.

Kayla was pacing back and forth, still a little wobbly in her knees from the adrenaline. "Sure—you're so soft-hearted, the post-hypnotic suggestion wouldn't have held for more than five minutes. I was going out of my mind as it were when these two dummies started to look like they might back out at the last moment."

"Well, that's all the thanks you get for chivalry!" exclaimed Rastus.

Elan was giving out hugs. "We had to build in a few doubts to make it look realistic, and they aren't really chivalrous, you know."

Kayla dropped her cup. "They're coming for us!"

"Who?"

"Them," said Nessa pointing at what Kayla had sensed. The door slid open and a stream of uniformed armed men came rushing into the room.

"On the ground, nobody move!" shouted the leader.

Caius protested, "This is a private residence! You can't come bursting in here!"

Two of the men grabbed him and pulled him roughly to the floor. Before they could do anything else, Silas picked them both up and threw them bodily across the room. He turned to deal similarly with the rest of the intruders but was interrupted by Elan.

"Stop Silas, they might shoot, and they aren't carrying stun guns."

He paused for a second and realized they were carrying assault rifles, lethal at any range. Before he could decide what to do, they were on him. He relaxed to let them handcuff him rather than to risk one of the rifles go off and kill someone.

He heard Elan call out, "Stop!" and then lost consciousness as something hit his head.

Silas awoke to find himself in a small, featureless room. The walls were plain metal, with only the thin mattress he was lying on for furniture. His head throbbed painfully when he sat up.

"Hello?" he thought.

No one answered. He couldn't seem to find anyone. That was odd. That was *very* odd. Maybe the bump on the head had left him a little weak? The door was little more than a featureless seam; it didn't seem to give much hope for escape, but he made the effort, on principle, to try forcing it open. Bruising his fingers, he returned to the mattress to think.

It looked like Alceron workmanship, so he was probably still on his home planetoid, or possibly one of the others. As far as he knew, no mechanical device could block MT, so the lack of response was very strange. Possibly someone had developed a blocking system that was still top secret.

"Silas, are you awake yet?"

"Kayla! Boy, is it good to hear you. How come I can't contact anyone?"

"We're in the palace cells. There are guards trained to block MT to stop prisoners plotting and escaping. Luckily they aren't very strong, but I can still only go a few rooms in either direction. You should be able to reach Rastus, if you try hard enough. He's in the room next to you."

"Are the others okay?"

"Yep. Is your head okay?"

"Sure, it's fine."

"Good. I told the others it was more likely that the rifle they hit you with was damaged. I'll check back on you in a few minutes."

CHAPTER THIRTEEN

Calron disappeared into another room, leaving Jaros on his own for a moment. Jaros was rather jumpy. When Calron started making vague wishy-washy statements about the future, it was usually a good time to panic. At least Kayla and Elan would be safe back on the ship.

The robot trundled back into the room and said, "Come on then, we'll miss the ship if we don't get a move on. I don't know how humans survived without comps to keep reminding them of things."

"But you were the one we were waiting for."

"Have it your own way."

The lift started up towards the surface, gathering speed slowly. Jaros kept his eye on Calron, waiting to see what he would do next, but he remained silent until the lift had almost stopped.

"I think you should know that I've activated the self-destruct sequence to destroy this base in a few minutes. It should be quite safe, only a little explosion. We wouldn't want the Gronch to find it."

By the time the doors slid open, Jaros was certain the robot had finally flipped. He hurried up onto the edge of the crater just in time to see their ship vanishing into space.

When the robot arrived he was sitting on the edge of the crater looking up at the sky. "It left without us."

Watching the robot scan the horizon by slowly rotating its head in a complete circle gave Jaros a sore neck. He tried unsuccessfully to rub his neck through his space suit.

"They have left," the robot stated redundantly.

"And?" prompted Jaros in hope of hearing a brilliant plan.

"And one of us is going to run out of oxygen in approximately twenty three-minutes."

"Not before he's dismantled the other one!"

"There's no need to get violent. I've already discovered a way to save your life."

"Well?" prompted Jaros, taking the bait.

"Well what?"

"How are you going to save my life?"

"You don't really want to know, now do you? Wouldn't you rather wait and be surprised?"

"No, tell me now."

The robot hesitated. "You're not going to like it."

Jaros fixed the robot in a hard stare. "I already don't like it. You're stringing me along just to keep me happy for my last remaining minutes."

"I wouldn't do that, Jaros."

"Why not?"

"Because it would be against my programming to lie."

"How do I know you aren't just saying that?"

"You think I would fib to a man with only twenty-one minutes to live?"

"Ah ha!" said Jaros smugly, "I was right! You just admitted I am still going to die."

"No, I didn't."

"Yes, you did!"

"Maybe I did that on purpose, just to keep you occupied."

"Why would you want to do that?"

"So you wouldn't run away, hide and eventually die of asphyxiation before we could be captured by those two Gronch soldiers."

Jaros turned around just in time to look surprised for a second before the gigantic ugly creature picked him up by one leg. "I'll get you for this," he shouted back at Calron, before the alien plodded back to the ship that had landed in the silence of vacuum a few meters away.

"I knew he wouldn't like it," said Calron to himself as the other Gronch carried him towards the ship.

Walking back to his ship, Grumm tried not to drop the horrible gangly creature, but it was difficult to keep a hold on its smooth, slippery spacesuit. The Gronch guard wondered what sort of outlandish environment could have caused a creature to evolve with thin, featureless skin and long spindly limbs. All the horrible stories appeared true. He could see no tail, not even a short one!

Grumm was not very happy, even for a Gronch. A career in the space fleet had seemed so promising, but with such a low MT rating he was beginning to realize that promotion was not to be his lot. And now, to compound his misfortune, he was expected to take care of these ugly little creatures.

Jaros fell slowly to the floor when the Gronch released him. In normal gravity he would have been hurt, but luckily the ship was still resting on the moon's surface.

Moments later, Calron was thrown in and Jaros was forced to dodge quickly to avoid injury.

"Here's a spot of luck!" said the robot unexpectedly as he picked himself off the floor.

"That's an interesting statement, coming from a prisoner on an alien spaceship."

"I was referring to the fact that we have been placed in the same cell."

"You mean there's some chance of escape as long as we're together?"

"No," laughed the robot. "Not the slightest, but at least we'll have each other to talk to."

"I can hardly wait," said Jaros crossly.

"Now, don't be negative. You should try to cultivate an optimistic attitude towards life's little setbacks."

"Little setbacks! Have you been reading human books again?"

"There's nothing wrong with trying to broaden one's horizons, even for a being with my tremendous intellect. Anyway, as I was saying, positive thinking is the secret to success, for humans anyway."

"I have broad enough horizons already. For example, I remember reading that depression is a much saner state of mind. Someone conducted a study which showed that depressed people are better at judging the likelihood of future events."

"It's very easy to predict failure and then fulfil your own prophecy by not even trying. But in fact, you're right; it's perfectly logical when weighing the pros and cons to decide that logically speaking, the chances of success are so slim it's not worth the risk of trying. But where would we be if the inventor of the space drive had thought like that, or even the inventor of the telephone? How many things would never have been done if people didn't try even though the odds were against them?"

Jaros felt sure he'd heard something similar once before. "So what you're trying to say is that the one thing a human absolutely can't afford to have is an accurate sense of perspective? We have to be illogical to function?"

"Well, it's not illogical, really."

Jaros knew better than to continue arguing with Calron. "Okay, I give up!"

"But that's the whole point — giving up is the problem."

Jaros sat up and stretched just enough so he could kick the robot, damaging his toe in the process. "Ouch."

Just then the guard reappeared at the door.

"I've come to question you before your execution," he said, and then added, *"Resistance is useless!"*

"What did it say?" asked Calron, who couldn't hear telepathic speech.

"It said it's going to kill us, after asking a few questions."

"Open your mind, puny creature."

Jaros ignored it.

"What are you telling it?"

"Nothing, of course."

"Oh!" said Calron, a little surprised. "Don't you think it would be wiser to talk?"

"No."

"But if you don't talk, it's going to kill us."

"Better that, than betraying the whole human race."

"Ah, it's your conscience that is bothering you. What a nuisance. I don't have one, you know. It makes life much easier. How about if you just tell it who we are, that won't be giving anything much away, and there's a good chance it will take us to someone higher up before killing us."

"Then what will we do?"

"I don't know. I'm sure I'll come up with something by then. I am terribly clever, you know."

"Could have fooled me!"

Grumm was getting very agitated. He knew his MT was pretty low, but he hadn't realized how low until he bounced off Jaros' shield. Any other Gronch might have suspected something, but Grumm was just worried. If anyone else found out about this, he'd never be able to swing his tail in public again. He tried to think of a way out of the problem. Unfortunately thinking was his other weak suit; but after a few moments he managed to devise a plan. If the creature were dead, then no one would be able to prove he hadn't questioned it. The more he thought about his plan, the more he liked it. His plotting was interrupted.

"Ok, I'll talk. I'm the Prince of Alceron and this is the computer Calron who's been plotting to destroy the Gronch Empire."

Grumm was furious. The first time he'd managed to come up with a really clever plan and now it was going to have to be completely rethought. If he killed them, and they were who they said they were, then sooner or later someone would probably figure it out and he'd be in for it. On the other hand, if they were lying and he brought them to his superior, then everyone would know that the creature had a stronger mind. On the third hand—Grumm counted his hands and frowned for a minute. On the third hand, he continued stubbornly, if they were telling the truth and he brought them to his superior's attention, they might still reveal that they hadn't been probed.

Grumm rubbed his head. It hurt from the unaccustomed effort.

"What's wrong?" asked Jaros, sensing that the huge ugly creature had a problem.

That's odd, thought Grumm; it seems to be concerned about me! *"I was supposed to probe your mind."*

"So?"

"Do you think you might not mention to anyone that I didn't?"

"I doubt the topic will come up," replied Jaros, but the creature still radiated nervousness so he added, *"But if anyone asks, you did just what you were supposed to."*

"Oh, good," concluded Grumm and left, still a little worried that he hadn't thought everything through properly.

After two days in captivity, Jaros came to the conclusion that Calron didn't particularly mind being glowered at, so he started ignoring him instead.

Calron's lower housekeeping systems continued with their normal business, scanning memory storage, cross-referencing and reorganizing data when necessary or possible. His higher cognitive networks were considering various problems and estimating possible outcomes.

Suddenly, a hardware error alerted one of the lower processors. It scanned the affected memory unit and then sent an alert up to the main logic circuit. Calron's logic circuit brought the cognitive networks in to consider the problem. Luckily, it was a small memory area that contained only a few housekeeping systems. Calron marked the area as faulty and recovered the lost programs from his backups. Having solved the problem, he went back to what he had been thinking about.

A short while later, Grumm appeared for the second time that day. The first was to inform them that they would be kept alive until the Emperor had seen them. This second visit, also brief, was to deliver a meal for Jaros.

After the guard had left Jaros stared down at the platter with open hostility.

A small probe extended from Calron's hand into the substance.

"It's quite safe: a very healthy mixture actually. It should put some hair on your chest."

Jaros continued to stare at the repulsive-looking substance. "I'm not very hungry."

"Rubbish, of course you are." Calron knew humans sometimes got embarrassed about their bodily functions. "Don't mind me. Eat up. Enjoy."

Jaros picked up the odd looking spoon-like utensil, ladled up a chunk of the stuff and lifted it toward his nose. He sniffed at it suspiciously for a moment, closed his eyes and took a bite.

His eyes snapped open; the stuff was absolutely delicious. He couldn't believe it. He took another large spoonful and rolled it around in his mouth. It tasted like a mixture of chocolate cake and warm donuts, but not as sickeningly sweet as either. "Are you sure this stuff's good for me?"

"Positive; it's a perfectly balanced meal."

"Do you think you could reproduce it from your analysis?"

Calron considered this request for a moment. "You are asking the most intelligent computer in the galaxy if it can cook?"

"Yes, that's what I'm asking. What's the answer?"

"I'm not sure. I think so."

"Good."

Calron was interrupted again, this time from his background consistency task; not serious, but still worth investigating. It had found an apparent error in a reference to his total memory capacity. The robot considered how this could have occurred. When the value was stored, it would have been checked, and if it had been corrupted while it was stored, then the memory error detection circuitry should have alerted him.

This sort of error simply couldn't have happened! Calron didn't like this at all. He'd read about humans feeling that their minds were playing tricks on them, and now he was beginning to understand what it meant. For want of something better to do, he set a few more tasks going to check for other consistency errors and dedicated one cognitive circuit to try to come up with any other plausible explanations.

"We seem to have arrived," announced Jaros.

"How do you know?"

"I can sense it; there are lots of minds about— millions."

"Can you pick up anything interesting?"

Jaros looked a little shocked. "You mean eavesdropping?"

"Yes."

In Alceron's otherwise freethinking society, snooping on other people's thoughts was a strict and necessary taboo. Jaros had learned at an early age that the thoughts of others were not only private, but that they were not always pleasant, either. But his morals suddenly seemed a little out of place. With some effort he started to spread a web of feelers through the ether, being careful not to alert any of the minds of his presence.

"They can't last more than a few more weeks."

"How have they lasted this long? More than half the empire's fleet has been chasing after their ships for more than fifty years."

"Their ships are very difficult to hit, and all attempts at MT control have failed; they seem utterly immune. If they would stand and fight we could wipe them out in five minutes; but they keep running away and then attacking again at the most unlikely times. All attempts to analyse their strategy have failed."

"But you think you've got them now?"

"We're certain of it sir. Their numbers are dwindling and it seems probable they will put up one more concerted attack before we wipe them out entirely."

"Make sure you don't fail; our lives depend on it."

Jaros told Calron what he had heard.

"So, we have allies," said Calron.

"For the moment, at least."

"Then we'd better do our best to see that the moment lasts."

"We're not in the best position to be saving another alien race or anyone at all."

"Don't talk twaddle. We're in the heart of the Gronch Empire; what better place could there be?"

"The other side of that steel door would be nice," replied Jaros.

Just then their guard appeared at the door and hustled them out into the passage.

Grumm hurried the aliens along with an occasional prod with his rifle. He was letting them walk freely to avoid touching them again. It also improved his chances of being able to slip away before actually meeting the emperor, which in turn improved his chances of living another day. Sure enough, when they reached the outer waiting room an overzealous guard took charge of the prisoners and instructed Grumm to wait outside.

Jaros and Calron entered the dimly lit room. A turgid smell rose from the damp green walls, creating a very unpleasant atmosphere.

Jaros' step faltered as a mind probe hit his shields unexpectedly. Jaros recovered immediately and the probe ricocheted harmlessly away toward the hapless guard standing behind them. The guard sank to his knees as the remains of the spent mind probe hit him.

Graator stared down at them, outwardly calm and relaxed. Inside he was becoming mildly concerned. Certainly a high-ranking Gronch could deflect a mind probe, but for an alien to manage it!

"So you two small creatures are the great threat to the Gronch Empire?"

"That's correct," replied Jaros.

"Your metallic friend isn't even telepathic?"

"No, but that hasn't stopped him from causing the imminent fall of your empire."

Several members of the Gronch entourage began to twitch their tails nervously. Graator could be very unpredictable when he got angry.

"How exactly is he going to manage that?" asked Graator, apparently still calm.

"I'm afraid I can't tell you that. All I can say is that the Gronch race will no longer be tolerated outside its home solar system. If you don't withdraw your forces immediately, we shall be forced to exterminate your entire race." Jaros paused for effect. *"However, in our infinite mercy, we are prepared to give you the opportunity to surrender and avoid any unnecessary bloodshed."*

Graator started to shake with rage. Nobody had ever spoken to him in this way. The mental instability that had led to his unusually high MT rating also resulted in a rather short temper. Before he could stop himself, one of the servants had exploded in a ball of flame. Jaros pretended not to notice as the other servants quickly extinguished the fire and started to clear away the mess. Clearly, they were not wholly unprepared for this kind of occurrence.

Graater came to a decision. He smiled viciously, making an otherwise ugly face appear considerably more frightening, *"Torture and death are too good for you."*

Turning to another of the Gronches Graater thought, *"Gerndt, take these aliens and a dozen battle cruisers and don't come back until the last of their race is dead. Make sure this one,"* Graator pointed his claw at Jaros, *" lives long enough to see his home planet die."*

"But sir, to do that I'll have to take seven or eight ships out of the war zone. One would be more than enough."

"ONE HAS ALREADY BEEN DESTROYED!" shouted Graator. *"AND THE MATTER WAS NOT UP FOR DISCUSSION!"*

"How's it going Jaros?" asked Calron, who could only observe the body language and guess at what was being said. "He seems to be a little volatile."

"Not well. Ssh."

"May your death be slow and painful, earthling," said Graator, dismissing them both.

They were dragged back out the way they had come in, where Grumm again took charge escorting them back to their cell.

"It's the last time I follow your advice," raved Jaros, after he had repeated what he could remember of the interview. "At least Earth and Alceron had a chance before; now they will be wiped out before a defence can be planned."

Calron waited patiently for Jaros to lose a little steam. "So you don't think the fact that we have drawn a little heat off our alien allies is at least a small accomplishment? Something you didn't think we could achieve only a few hours ago?"

"A hell of a lot of good that's going to do. It's not going to take more than a few days for them to wipe us out entirely. Then what good will we be to these allies?"

"Oh, I don't know about that. Apparently, we've already knocked out one of their battle cruisers and that was without the two of us," the robot reminded Jaros.

CHAPTER FOURTEEN

*F*inally, the Fleet Commander's secretary signalled them to enter. Although well liked, Mark had heard that the commander had something of a reputation for being a little eccentric.

"Stringer and Harwood, sir," said Alex as they both entered the Commander's office and stood rigidly to attention.

"Well lads, I don't think I've had the pleasure of meeting you two before. You look like a couple of good men. I expect you're going to make really fine officers one day. What brings you to my office?"

"We're the volunteers," prompted Mark.

"Oh, yes, I remember." The warm smile disappeared from the Commander's face for a moment. "Are you sure? It could be frightfully dangerous."

Mark was about to voice his doubts when the commander suddenly continued. "Still, I guess you know what you're about. It's certainly not my job to talk you out of it. Now, what do you know about the mission so far?"

"Not a lot, sir. Well, nothing actually."

"Nothing!" the Commander sounded surprised, and then he remembered. "Oh, it's top secret, isn't it?"

"Yes, sir," agreed Alex.

"It all started after that attack from the aliens," the Commander paused, wondering why he kept wanting to give them a name, but the word refused to come out of his mouth. "Bit of a thrashing all round; so, as soon as the survivors from the space attacks had been picked up, we sent out most of the fleet in the hope of finding something upon which to take a little revenge."

"No luck?" asked Alex.

"No, none at all, which is probably lucky if the reports describing the way the aliens manoeuvre and accelerate is even half true."

He continued: "Anyway, they seemed to have left the system entirely. But then, some of the boffins on the moon started picking up a weak radio signal coming from the asteroid belt. At first we thought it might be a distress signal from an Earth ship that got stranded in the confusion. But according to the boffin brigade, the signal is not of earthly origin."

"And you want us to go out and have a look at it?" asked Mark.

"Yes, but there is one more thing you should know."

"What's that?"

"You won't be the first ones to go. I'm afraid we haven't heard anything from the first ship we sent; it's lost, all hands presumed dead."

The commander watched the young lads leave his office. He had a nagging feeling there was something he ought to remember. He also had a suspicion that they shouldn't be messing around with whatever the aliens had left behind. But you couldn't run a space fleet on intuition. It was such a pity; they seemed awfully young, those two. Far too young to… His superstitious nature stopped him from finishing the sentence.

Within a few days, Mark and Alex were aboard a carrier travelling at sub light speed toward the asteroid belt, their own tiny ship secured in the cargo hold. For the first couple of days Mark had hung around the main lounge hoping to catch a glimpse of Doctor Hayes.

Hayes wasn't just a scientist; he was "THE SCIENTIST" in capital letters. He first became well known when he rescued physics from the 30-year embarrassment that followed the experiments of a smart aleck young student who couldn't resist proving that relativity wasn't.

Doctor Hayes' theory not only explained the annoyingly non-relative results but also explained a good deal more, besides. His work led directly to the building of the reaction less space drive.

Of course, some people claimed he was past his prime, or even that he'd lost his marbles altogether. And, rumours that he spent his time chasing around after UFO sightings hadn't helped his already flaky image. But Mark didn't care. He'd admired Hayes for years, and now he had a chance to meet the living legend in the flesh; but so far the good doctor didn't seem to be the sociable sort. Hanging about in the main lounge hadn't resulted in even a single sighting. Still, on a ship this size, Mark felt he was certain to bump into him sooner or later.

Alex didn't seem to be enjoying the trip much. He had a morbid tendency to dwell on the good prospects they both had for an untimely demise.

"Cheer up, Alex. I told you Kayla would fix things."

"Great. I'm about to face almost certain death and my partner is hearing voices. Yes, that helps a lot."

"The last ship might have had an accident, crashed into one of the asteroids, perhaps. Space gets pretty crowded out there."

"Crowded, huh? No it doesn't! The chances of them having hit something are next to zero, even if they were stupid enough to turn off their automatic avoidance system."

"Something else might have happened, though; and they were all alone in a single ship, whereas we have this entire carrier backing us up."

"So, anyway, what have these voices advised us to do?"

Mark cleared his throat, "Well, I haven't heard from Kayla since the other night. But she said she'd get back to me again really soon. I'm sure she will before we get there."

"Great!" said Alex again, and he lapsed into silence.

Crowding onto the bridge, they all watched the giant central vid screen. It displayed the surface of the asteroid a large glowing arrow pointed to a tiny speck, which someone had identified as the missing ship. Another glowing arrow pointed out the source of the radio signal. It was an equally featureless speck.

The expedition leader was speaking. "Our two brave lads will land their craft here." He pointed to a spot respectably distant from the beacon. "Assuming all goes well, they will approach the fleet ship by foot and try to establish the whereabouts of its crew."

Mark was examining the faces of the various scientists and techs in the room when he recognized Doctor Hayes. He was a little shorter than Mark had expected and seemed much older; all the film clips Mark had seen of Hayes had been taken years earlier.

"Will they be carrying vid and audio transmitters?" asked one of the techs.

"Yes. If something happens we'll know what not to do next time; not that anything's going to happen," Dr. Hayes finished, remembering that Mark and Alex were on the bridge with the group.

Mark clambered into his suit. "Testing, testing, do you read?"

"Loud and clear."

"Video?"

"Just fine."

Normally the backpack would have weighed Mark down, but on the asteroid it simply made movement more difficult. Alex appeared out of the air lock and drifted up into the air, his attempt to step down to the ground producing a little too much upward thrust. A quick burst from the gas jets in his suit reversed his drift.

"Where's the ship?" Alex asked as he touched onto the asteroid's surface.

"Over that way," replied Mark, pointing to a small mark on the horizon. "I figure about ten steps if we're careful not to go into orbit."

Mark let his body fall slowly forward until his face was only a foot off the ground, and then pushed gently with his feet. He sailed slowly forward and couldn't resist saying, "Up, up, and away," quietly to himself.

"Say again?" came a voice in his ear. "We didn't quite read your transmission."

"Sorry. I was just clearing my throat."

As they neared the ship a few minutes later, Mark slowed and then stopped himself after a few contacts with the surface. He waited twenty meters from the ship as Alex, who had lost the toss, approached it. Alex slowly made his way around the ship before disappearing into the air lock.

"They aren't here," Alex reported.

"What about the suits?" asked one of the techs from the carrier.

"Two gone."

"Any log entries?"

After a pause: "Nothing after they landed."

"Okay. Move on to the beacon."

Minutes later, Alex stood next to Mark not more than fifty meters from the beacon. A barely visible spherical haze shimmered around what appeared to be some sort of ship. Two humanoid figures were on the ground at the edge of the haze. Mark approached this time, leaving Alex to watch nervously from behind a boulder.

As he approached the figures he recognized the suits. Then a moment later he recognized the contorted faces within. They were the crew of the fleet ship, both dead.

The bodies lay on the ground, partially within the haze. Mark peered at their suits from a few feet away for some sign of damage but found none. Finally he knelt closer to read the gauges; both air tanks were empty. Mark started to examine one of the suits for some other sign of injury, when his hand brushed against the haze. It stuck instantly! In the attempt to pull free in the light gravity, he brought his knee into contact. It stuck too!

"Alex, I need help."

"What's happened?"

"I'm stuck."

"Huh?"

"I'm stuck to this force field, or whatever it is. It doesn't hurt. It just won't let go. Be careful not to touch it when you approach."

Alex crept up the last few paces. "What should I do?"

"Pull me out, dummy."

"Oh, okay." He gingerly took hold of Alex's suit and tried to pull but only succeeded in pulling himself toward Mark. "I need something to push against."

They both looked at the dusty ground for a second before noticing the body. "He won't mind."

Alex grabbed hold of a lifeless limb with one hand and Mark with the other and pulled. For a moment nothing seemed to happen and then suddenly Mark's hand came free. "It's working! Keep pulling." A moment later his knee came loose and they fell backwards, away from the force field.

"This is Mark. It's all clear down here. You can bring down some tech guys to check this thing out."

A voice from the ship asked, "Is it safe? What killed those two?"

"I expect they got stuck like me, only they pulled each other further into the field and eventually died when their air ran out."

CHAPTER FIFTEEN

After two days of saying very little, Calron suddenly turned to Jaros and announced: "I think it's about time we escaped. We should be nearing Alceron soon."

"Oh, great idea. How do you plan to do that?"

"I don't. I thought I'd leave the details to you. Long-term planning and seeing the whole picture are more my line."

"And what does your long-term plan say we should do, assuming we do get out of this cell, in the middle of a Gronch battle cruiser? Will we single-handedly overpower several thousand Gronch troupers?"

"I didn't mean escape from the cell. Heavens, no! That would be suicide. I meant we should escape from this ship so we can get back to Alceron in time to give a little warning."

Jaros gave up. Calron didn't seem to process sarcasm; or he pretended not to, anyway. Jaros paced back and forth in the small cell, trying to think of a brilliant plan of escape. Alas, nothing seemed to spring to mind. Then he remembered a few stray thoughts he'd caught earlier.

"Grumm?" he called.

"Who is that? Oh, it's you. What do you want, alien?"

"I just wanted to chat with someone; do you mind?"

Grumm considered this request. Could it be a trick? Probably, but at least it might be interesting. *"Okay. I'll be down in a minute."*

After quickly finishing off the remains of his ample meal Grumm dropped the empty containers into a disposal unit and trudged down to the prisoner's cell.

"Here I am!" He announced upon his arrival. *"Go on, then, chat away."*

"How's life been treating you lately, Grumm?"

"Huh? You want to talk about me?"

"Of course. It isn't often I get to meet a Gronch; and any break from this tin can I'm rooming with is a pleasant break. So, how's life?"

"Not bad," replied Grumm cautiously. *"Well, it's not all that good actually. In fact, come to think of it, life's a bit of a drag, really."*

"Really?" returned Jaros with surprise. *"I would have thought a bright young officer like you would be enjoying himself, seeing the galaxy, meeting interesting creatures, blowing up the enemy."*

"Yes," agreed Grumm, his eyes lighting up. *"It certainly sounds exciting enough, and I suspect if I was an officer I might like the job. But the way things are now I seem to get all the really unpleasant jobs: grubby, messy, dull tasks no one else wants—no offence intended, of course. Being in orbit around an exotic planet in a faraway system threatening to destroy their entire civilization isn't as much fun when you're stuck inside the bowels of the ship, knee deep in refuse, trying to unblock a drain."*

"Yes, I can see how that wouldn't be very satisfying," commiserated Jaros.

"I should have been promoted by now but my MT is not very, ah, consistent. I know I could score higher, if I had half a chance."

"A pity you weren't born on Alceron, really."

"How do you figure that?"

"Back there you'd have one of the highest ratings in the system. I expect you'd be a general or something of the sort."

Grumm's brain grappled with this new concept; there was a place where his innate abilities would be considered exceptional, instead of pitiful. It was a little hard to believe. *"I think I'd better be going now. I've got some work to do."*

"Okay, it's been nice talking with you."

"What were you talking to it about?" asked Calron when the Gronch had gone.

"I was simply arranging our escape, just as you asked me."

"With our guard?"

"Yes."

"Don't you think that's a little unwise?" inquired the robot.

"I seem to remember that I was made head of the escape committee. Unless you want to take over the job, I suggest you stop bothering me with silly questions so I can get on with it."

"Pardon me for breathing, which of course I don't."

Jaros was jolted from his sleep to find two enormous leathery hands shaking him violently back and forth. He was quickly wide-awake.

"Are you awake?" asked Grumm.

"Yes, what do you want?"

"I'm going to desert and I thought you might like to come with me."

Jaros quivered at the thought that the dumb creature might have left without them. *"That sounds like a good idea."*

They stumbled along the dim passages of the ship, Jaros and Calron in front and Grumm bringing up the rear with a blaster pointed at them for effect. At first no one seemed to take any notice, but then one of the Gronch guards must have scanned Grumm.

"Stop and die!" shouted the guard, not being one for thinking through the basic principles of threatening.

Grumm froze from force of habit, but a solid kick in the leg from Jaros brought him back to his senses. The alien giant then scooped up the robot with one enormous arm and sprinted down the passage with Jaros struggling to keep up. Blaster fire exploded above their heads as they rounded another corner. Grumm stopped and shot off a couple of blasts to keep their pursuers at bay while he lifted a large square metal plate from the floor and jumped into the darkness below. Jaros peered into the blackness doubtfully for a second before following.

He landed with a splash, ankle deep in something slimy. *"Come on Earthling, they may try to follow,"* said Grumm, roughly grabbing Jaros by the arm, dragging him forward through the darkness.

Jaros followed along helplessly, doing his best to keep on his feet and avoid falling into the slime.

"This is the last time I leave a human to organize something," complained Calron from over Grumm's shoulder.

"I don't know what you're complaining about. I'm the one who has to walk through this mess. At least we're outside our cell and we haven't been captured yet!"

"I assume you know where we are?"

"Well, no, I don't. But Grumm seems to know where he's going. I expect we'll arrive somewhere soon."

Jaros was wrong. They didn't arrive anywhere soon. Nearly an hour had passed before Grumm finally stopped. Jaros' eyes, which had by now adjusted to the gloom, could make out claw holds leading up the wall. At the top, there was another of the metal plates.

"We're just below the hanger deck. You'd better have a peek out to see if the coast is clear," directed Grumm.

Jaros climbed up the wall and bent his shoulder to the metal plate above and pushed. Nothing happened. He pushed a harder; still nothing. It was obviously made for a Gronch, not a human. He adjusted his footing and heaved upwards. The plate lifted a few inches and Jaros peered out into the brilliant light before its weight brought the cover back down.

"It looks deserted," he reported.

"Good. Follow me. We need to get to one of the scout ships. They are faster, so we won't be caught."

Watching the alien, Jaros began to re-evaluate his opinion; it apparently wasn't as dumb as he thought. It bounded up the wall still holding Calron in one arm and effortlessly lifted the plate with its other claw before stepping out onto the floor above. Jaros followed as quickly as he could; when he got to the top Grumm and Calron were already disappearing into an air lock. Jaros dived after them, just pulling his feet in before the door slid shut.

The giant's face was looking down at him pityingly. *"How did your ancestors survive? Weak and helpless, you must have been easy prey for every meat-eating predator."*

"We got really good at running away," explained Jaros. *"Practically no other animal on earth can swim rivers, run for miles and climb trees."*

"What's a tree?" asked Grumm as the inner lock door slid open.

Jaros would have answered but a huge angry wall of green came thundering towards them. The ship was apparently not empty. Jaros stepped into the oncoming rush and packed his best punch solidly in the alien's face. Unfortunately, Gronch were not particularly sensitive in the facial region; the fleshy green skin numbly absorbed Jaros' attack.

The Gronch didn't recognize him as the enemy and simply brushed Jaros aside, throwing him sprawling across the room. Calron dropped to the floor, forgotten. Grumm leapt at the attacker with a blood-curdling roar. Jaros and Calron watched as the two giants thrashed around the room. Within seconds the fight was over and the victim lay on the floor, dead.

Jaros didn't move. By the time he'd recovered from his fall he had lost track of who was who.

"Grumm?" he asked cautiously.

"I enjoyed that. He deserved to die, that one." Turning away from the body, Grumm thought, *"You'd better be getting us into space. They will be breaking down the hatch in a few minutes."*

Jaros examined the alien controls. *"I think you better pilot it."*

"I'm not a pilot. Why do you think I brought you? And you'll have to break the computer lock, too. I presume this tin can I've been carrying can manage that?"

"Of course it can. It's the cleverest computer system that ever existed. I expect it can fly the ship too."

"I think there's something you should know," replied Calron after Jaros had explained the problem.

"What?" Jaros asked with suspicion.

"I'm not Calron."

"What? Then who the hell are you?"

"I don't currently know who or what I am. I have established that I'm not the Calron you know. But whether I was built by him, if he even exists, or even if I was built by someone else, I just don't know."

"How long have you been keeping this little secret to yourself?"

"Only the last day or so. I didn't want to depress you while we were still prisoners."

"And how is it that you took so long to figure out that you weren't Calron? Surely you should have noticed the deficiencies within seconds?"

"I note that you didn't, and anyway, I was programmed not to notice. My auto-checking procedures were all patched in such a way to prevent the inconsistencies from being reported. If it wasn't for a freak memory failure, which forced me to use some backup procedures, which apparently hadn't been patched, I probably never would have realized."

"So you won't be able to hotwire this ship?"

"Oh, I don't know about that. I may not be Calron, but I'm still a lot brighter than your average block of wood."

"Well, get on with it then."

"Aye, aye, Captain."

Jaros turned back to Grumm, who was standing with his foot in the air lock door to prevent it from closing. The ship started to reverberate with the impacts of some large object on the other lock door.

"Will they be able to get through?"

"Yes— in a few seconds, probably."

Jaros didn't quite believe it until he saw the bulges begin to appear in the metal door. "Come on, Calron, we need to leave. Now!"

"Very well, but I can't guarantee anything if you insist on rushing me."

"That doesn't matter; anywhere is better than here."

A claw forced its way through the tiny gap at the side of the buckling outer door and began to tear the metal apart. Grumm stepped back to allow the inner door to close; and then they were suddenly falling upward when the small ship disconnected from the battle cruiser.

"Nice one, Calron."

"One does try one's best," replied Calron as their ship accelerated into space. "If you don't mind. I would prefer it if you called me something else. That name doesn't seem appropriate anymore."

"Oh, all right. Ummm…" Jaros considered some of the more popular comp names: Robbie was a well over-used. How about Bob? No, that doesn't sound right. Maybe something more exotic, like Hinsch or Mocom. I know, how about `Jowett?' How does that sound?"

"That will do nicely."

CHAPTER SIXTEEN

*E*lan was escorted into an adjoining room. The room contained a single table in the centre and a chair. Ranic was sitting casually on the edge of the table.

"Have a seat Elan. Relax."

Elan folded her arms and didn't move. "I'd rather stand, thanks all the same."

"Have it your own way."

"You realize we are being illegally held? You'll never get away with it!"

"Get away with what? Imprisoning a bunch of suspected traitors during a state of war?"

"Traitors!" Elan's anger was getting the best of her. "We single-handedly wiped out that Gronch battle cruiser and you have the nerve to call us the traitors?"

"Ah, that was you, was it? I'd been wondering; thanks for clearing that up for me. Now I can take the credit without any fear of contradiction."

Elan wanted to kick herself. "If you didn't know that, then why are we here?"

"You're here, along with fifty or sixty others, because you are suspected of being royalists. Do you think I assumed power without anyone complaining?"

"Well, yes. What made you think we were royalists?"

"Me? The city comp produced the list, although, with your association with that Earth girl, I would have added your little family anyway. Now, since I'm the inquisitor and you are the respondent, what do you know about the Earth girl?"

"Nothing."

"Come, come. I don't want to lower myself to making threats of physical violence, but if I must...."

In a flash of inspiration Elan said, "It was you, wasn't it? You arranged for Jaros to get left on that moon?"

"I hardly think I should take all the credit; after all, his own stupidity certainly helped," replied Ranic with a wicked smile. "Now you were saying about Kayla?"

"I wasn't saying anything. You're obviously not going to let us go with what we know, so any further threats aren't very meaningful, are they?"

"Kayla? Tell the others we are not talking. Ignore all threats. If anyone gets a chance to take out a guard and escape, then take it. Ahrrghh..." Elan collapsed unconscious from the blow.

"Guards, take her back. No food or water for any of them. We'll see how stubborn they are in another day or two."

Whack!

Kayla woke instantly and looked towards the door for the source of the noise, but it was still closed. She turned around slowly, examining the tiny room and quickly discovering the source of the disturbance. A metal spike was protruding through the synthetic wall material. While she watched it slowly disappeared, leaving a small hole. A second later, something else protruded through the hole and a faint buzzing sound started. A circle about thirty centimetres across was slowly traced out of the wall. When it was completed, the section fell through.

Kayla peered into the darkness beyond. There wasn't much light, but she could make out the form of two small robots and several human figures. Elan's face appeared at the front, her eye swollen badly. "Kayla, are you alright? I couldn't contact you to warn you. Your mind block seemed to be up."

"Was it? Sorry, I was asleep."

Silas nudged Elan out the way. "Come on, we can't stand around and chat; the guards are bound to notice soon."

"I can't fit through this!" complained Kayla as Silas pulled her through.

"No problem," he said.

Kayla rubbed a couple of new bruises and Elan thumped Silas, "You dumb lout. She's not as tough as us. Earthlings bruise easier."

"Huh? I'm fine!" contradicted Kayla. She quickly hugged everyone.

A metallic voice cleared its throat. "We should be going."

The two small robots that appeared to be their saviours trundled off down the passage with the humans following.

"Who sent them?" asked Kayla.

"They don't know," replied Elan. "They're only constructor robots...not very bright."

Elan began to get nervous as they were led out into the public passageways. Someone was going to notice their absence soon, and then their faces would be appearing on every vid screen in Alceron. They boarded the stationary train. Elan waited the endless seconds before it started. If the broadcast came now, getting off could be tricky.

At long last the train stopped and they quickly filed off, still following the little robots. The station's vid screen, which usually showed timetables or advertising for the local shops, suddenly resolved to an image of a uniformed man.

"The traitors who betrayed Alceron's whereabouts to the Gronch have escaped. They are dangerous. If you see them, contact the palace immediately..."

Elan didn't hear any more as they hurried down a deserted passageway before their pictures were shown. They continued down back passageways and luckily, due to the late hour, not many people were about. The few people who did pass them obviously hadn't paid much attention to the announcement. Finally they arrived at what appeared to be a dead end passage, where a hinged wall panel swung neatly backwards and allowed them to enter.

Kayla followed the others through the panel and found herself in a large, messy room. Towels and odd items of clothing were scattered around. Some sort of mechanical device was partly dismantled on a bench. There was a place for everything, and pretty much everything was in something else's place.

Single men, she thought to herself. Drawing her eyes away from the disarray, Kayla became aware that everyone was staring at a tall, rather handsome, grey-haired man. Standing next to him was Breckin. He was beaming at Kayla, looking a little like a cat having just swallowed two canaries.

"I see you haven't lost any weight." said Kayla.

"I see you haven't gained any," he replied.

"So who's this?" asked Kayla gesturing towards the older man.

"Oh, I suppose you wouldn't know. This is Andrade, the late king of Alceron."

Andrade stepped forward with a flourish and kissed Kayla's hand, "An honour to meet you at last."

Kayla stood, speechless. Hearing his voice, his likeness to Jaros had suddenly jumped out at her.

Finally Caius managed to voice what the others were all thinking. "But you died in that accident on Alceron Three. We saw the newscasts. There was even a body!"

"At the risk of using a cliché, the reports of my death have been greatly exaggerated. I was only badly wounded, and when Calron pointed out that whoever was trying to kill me would eventually succeed given enough chances, we decided it would be best for me to stay dead. Anyway, it was good for Jaros to run things for a while."

Calron's shiny body appeared in the far door. "Chatter, chatter, chatter. It's a wonder humans ever get anything done. Here we are in the middle of a civil war, not to mention a galactic war, and you still take half an hour just to say hello."

"Oh shut up, Calron," said Kayla, and then felt rather awkward when everyone looked at her. "Oh, sorry, I didn't mean that." It had just come out like a reflex reaction, but even she knew that no one spoke to Calron like that.

Surprisingly, he didn't seem to take offence. "That's okay; but if you've finished the emotional reunion stuff, I think we should start making some plans."

The next morning Kayla stumbled back into the main workroom from one of the side rooms that had been hastily nominated as the women's dormitory. Elan and the two small robots were busily at work putting the room into some semblance of order.

"Good, someone finally stirs. Kayla, would you see what you can do with that bench over there?"

Kayla blinked twice and shook her head, trying to get rid of the sleepiness. "Why didn't the robots tidy up earlier?" she inquired while trying to decide at which end of the bench to start.

"I expect no one bothered to tell them to do it."

"Tell who to what?" asked Andrade, entering the room.

"Oh, nothing," said Elan.

"We we're just discussing how the place got in such a mess," said Kayla. "And why no one asked the robots to tidy up."

"Oh—is that why they weren't doing it?" Andrade sounded like he had just solved one of life's deepest mysteries. "I was wondering if there might be some trick to it."

CHAPTER SEVENTEEN

*T*he ship had been a flurry of activity for two days. Initially, Mark and Alex were used in place of white mice someone had forgotten to bring, pushing objects into the field to watch as they seemed just to hang in mid-air. Alex spent half an hour pushing to get the end of his finger into the field; after which, he had to spend another half hour tugging to get it back out. The extensive examinations, jabbing, and pulling did more damage to his finger than to the field. Convinced it was safe, the scientists brushed aside the young fleet officers so that the real work could begin.

Hayes seemed to be running things, with the top echelon of scientists running around helping him. They in turn had the other scientists and techs running around after them. Mark would have offered to help, but the only job still going was "tea boy." Eventually, even that seemed better than sitting around waiting. At least it got him close enough to eavesdrop and check out the thing they were building.

It was circular, about six feet across and made from metal tubes about two inches in diameter. Every few inches along the large tubes there were small ringlets. A web of wires ran from the ringlets into some sort of control system at the centre. The whole thing was built inside a large flexi-glass dome that had been inflated next to the field, with a tunnel running to the ship's air lock so that suits weren't required.

As always, Hayes was standing on a platform suspended over the mass of wiring, running tests on the circuits. He let others help with the physical construction but no one else was allowed anywhere near the control system. Mark overheard rumours that he had been working on it for over a year. In fact, one of the techs claimed that Hayes hardly left his cabin during the journey out because he was rushing to finish it before they arrived.

Alex claimed he heard some of the other scientists saying that they thought Hayes was using this strange field as an excuse to get the rest of his loony device constructed, but since none of them understood what he was up to none dared to speak up, for fear of revealing their own ignorance.

By the end of the second day the bustling work had come to an end. Only Hayes was left, suspended over his creation, patiently checking everything one more time.

Having lost the toss, Alex waited in his space suit for Mark to retreat a safe distance. The main spaceship was already drifting several kilometres above his head.

"Aren't you going to find some cover?" asked Alex when he saw Mark standing still.

"Huh? Oh, sorry. Yes, give me a moment."

Alex turned back to the Hayes device. Leading from the central unit was a thin cable that ended in a large switch. All he had to do was throw the switch. If it worked, Hayes claimed it would disrupt the force field around the alien ship. If it didn't work, then the techs seemed to be reasonably confident that the device itself, and everything in the near vicinity, would be atomised. Alex pondered what could well be his last remaining minutes of existence. Suddenly he wished he'd written a farewell note.

"Wake up, Stringer, we haven't got all day!"

"Yes, sir, I mean — no, sir." Alex looked around to check on Mark. The top of his helmet gleamed above a small boulder. Oh well, thought Alex, here goes nothing. He reached down to the large switch, took a deep breath and threw it. The device exploded instantly, throwing Alex backward.

The room eventually stopped spinning and the blurs looming above Alex resolved into white-coated humans. "I'm alive?"

"Certainly, once we fished you out of space. You're probably the first human to be blown into orbit!"

"What happened to Mark?"

"Don't worry, he's safely locked up," assured the Doctor.

Alex found his mind wasn't working very well. His thoughts seemed a little muddled. "Did you say locked up?"

"Yes, although Hayes and a good number of the science staff wanted to string him up on the spot; still everyone deserves to have their day in court."

"Mark is locked up?" Alex asked again, still certain he'd misunderstood some critical point.

The doctor tried to console him. "Yes, he's in the brig. You are quite safe now, he can't get to you."

Mark waited nervously outside the meeting room for his turn. Finally a clerk ushered him in. Three men sat behind a small bench: Mark's sergeant, a man he didn't recognize and Flynn, the patrol commander.

"Officer Harwood, you are charged with dereliction of duty, attacking a patrol officer, destroying patrol equipment, disobeying orders, and endangering the lives of other patrol officers. What have you to say on the matter?"

"I was only acting in the best interests of the patrol, sir."

"That is an interesting defence, young man. Would you care to explain?"

"I discovered that the force field we encountered was left by the Gronch. The weak radio transmissions were to lure us to that asteroid. Once there, our own inquisitive nature forced us to try to disable the field in the hope of discovering something useful from their ship."

The man Mark didn't recognize asked, "You seem to have discovered a great deal that eluded the best minds in the business. I suppose you can tell us what possible reason the aliens could have for wanting us to disable that force field?"

"It is basically a mouse trap, or maybe better described as a safety valve. The Gronch can't keep a constant eye on every tiny planet in the galaxy; instead, they leave these little toys near developing civilizations.

"A certain level of technology is required to disable the field. As soon as the field is disabled, the ship is released and takes off under automatic pilot heading directly for the sun, where, within a matter of hours, it induces a nova."

The sergeant interrupted, "I suppose you're going to tell us that every few days when our astronomers see another sun go nova it's really the consequences of an alien race reaching maturity and being destroyed as a result."

Mark paused and then said sadly, "I guess some of them probably are."

Flynn remained silent. He seemed rather preoccupied with something. Then he asked, "So I take it that you were only trying to destroy the machine built by Hayes and not intending to hit Alex Stringer when you started firing your blaster?"

"Yes, sir."

"And how is it that you come to know so much about galactic civilization?" asked the other man.

"That's rather a long story."

Flynn stood up. "Excuse me a minute, won't you?" he said and stepped out of the room. The other two looked at each other, not sure whether they should continue.

"We may as well go on. How do you explain the fact that this thing only just appeared? Shouldn't we have had one here already?"

"I don't know. Maybe the previous one had failed or maybe last time they were around here they didn't think any of the life forms showed promise of intelligence. Whatever the case, they obviously decided to leave one after that little skirmish a couple of weeks ago."

Flynn re-entered the room. Mark was stunned by his appearance. Although wearing the same clothes, he now looked several inches taller, his face looked younger, and when he spoke, his voice had none of the uncertainness of before.

"Well done, Harwood! You seem to have saved the Earth from certain destruction. Please report to patrol headquarters for a new assignment. Dismissed."

For a minute it looked like the sergeant was going to argue with Flynn, but the new authority in Flynn's manner was undeniable.

"Is Mark okay?" asked Elan.

"Yep. Calron was right. It all worked out. We cut it a bit close though; Mark fired just in time."

Calron looked up from the thing he was building. "I didn't realize Hayes was so near to creating an inertia-less field." He mumbled, "Fancy a human brain working out a thing like that? Wonders never cease."

"So what was the force field?" asked Kayla.

Calron answered, "Just a modified inertia less field generator. It had a very high internal inertia, instead of very low."

"Mule brain!" shouted Nessa over her shoulder as she stormed into the workroom.

Elan fixed her with a stern stare.

"It's Rastus. He won't give me a chance to use the console and we've only got the one in here."

"That's no excuse! You both spend too much time on that console anyway. What do you think people used to do before consoles were invented?"

"I don't know, what?" asked Nessa, entirely innocently.

Elan opened her mouth to speak and then shut it again, realizing that she didn't know. She looked at Kayla for help.

"Umm," said Kayla, sounding rather doubtful. "I think they used to watch vid shows a lot."

"Yes, there's an idea. Broaden your horizons and watch a few vid shows. There's a screen in the other room."

Nessa looked between them, not at all pleased that Rastus was getting away with something, and then stormed off into the other bedroom.

"They just don't like being cooped up," explained Elan. "It's an age thing."

"A good beating, that's what they need!" suggested Breckin.

"They're a bit old for that," said Kayla.

"True enough—you have to start beating them when they're young or it doesn't work."

"Did you do that with your kids?" asked Kayla.

"Ah, well, I guess not."

"Why not?"

"Don't know really," he mumbled, disappearing into the kitchen.

"What's wrong with him?" asked Kayla in a whisper, "Did I put my foot in something?"

Elan answered in hushed tones. "Possibly. I didn't know he had any kids; I've never heard him speak of any before. Maybe they died or something. Although, he looked more amused than upset. Shhh, here he comes."

Breckin slapped the robot cheerily on the back. "Come on, Calron. What's this thing you're making?"

"I'd rather not say."

"A secret weapon, eh? Something to help deal with those aliens, I'll bet," said Breckin enthusiastically.

"It's nothing of the sort."

"Then why won't you tell us what it is?" asked Kayla.

"Because it's a surprise!" stated Calron, refusing to say another word.

Kayla disappeared into the kitchen. Elan followed a few minutes later. She found Kayla busily clearing things away. "You've been avoiding it, haven't you!" stated Elan.

"What?" asked Kayla innocently, continuing to clear up the kitchen.

"Don't give me that. You've been running around like a lost goose doing every odd job you can find so you won't have any free time."

"I just like to do my share."

"Your share is to find out what Jaros is up to. I would have thought you couldn't wait to talk with him."

"I can't, but..."

"But, what?"

"It's just that," Kayla paused, "even though I said I'd know if he was hurt, well, I'm not so sure now. What if I try to find him and can't?"

"And what if he needs some help and you don't try to find him? Of all the hair-brained ideas!"

"But I could put him in danger. The Gronch might detect me!"

"Like hell they could. Now sit down and get on with it."

"Okay, okay. I can take a hint."

"Hi, lover boy!"

"What? Who said that?"

"Who said what?" asked Jowett.

Jaros looked at the robot for a second and then thought, *"Who said that?"*

"I'm offended! How many girls refer to you like that?"

"Kayla!"

"There's no need to shout. I'm not deaf!"

"Where are you? We're still light-years away!"

"I'm on Alceron."

"But that's impossible. You can't send from that distance!"

"Oh, sorry. I guess no one bothered to tell me."

"I've got some bad news. The Gronch are attacking in force. They are only a few hours behind me."

"Calron, Jaros says the Gronch fleet is on the way."

"Jolly good, nice to hear they are keeping to the schedule."

"Kayla, is Calron there with you?"

"Yep."

"Kick him for me, would you, darling?"

"Certainly, dear."

Thump.

Calron's head rotated down to look at his ankle and then at Kayla's obviously sore toe and then back at his ankle. "And most of the time they seem so rational," he mumbled to himself.

"Jaros, don't look now, but I think I can detect something else on your ship."

"What sort of thing?"

"An alien mind."

"Oh don't worry, that's only Grumm; he helped us escape. It's a long story."

"I've got time. Although, a gentleman might inquire after his betrothed when they have been apart for so long!"

"And give you a big head? Not likely!"

"Fine, then you can sit there by yourself."

Kayla withdrew to Alceron, intending to go back immediately, but, when she opened her eyes, she found the kitchen was now crowded with half the family there.

"Where is he?" asked Nessa.

"What's he been doing?" asked Rastus.

They all looked at her expectantly. Kayla felt a little silly and was about to make up an excuse when her thoughts were interrupted.

"Don't disappear when I'm about to apologize!"

"Jaros!" said Kayla and Elan together.

"I guess I never tried before. It's quite easy, really. Anyway you've missed out on the apology now. In fact, I think you owe me one!"

"I was just having a little fun!"

"Apology accepted."

"I wasn't apologizing."

"Of course not, dear."

"Just remember, when you get here you are going to suffer!"

"Will you two stop playing footsy for a second so we can get a decent report!" complained Elan.

"Sorry."

"Sorry."

"Bossy isn't she..."

"Shhh, you're at a safe distance; she could hit me."

Silas folded the piece of paper neatly and then tossed it into the air. It fluttered momentarily and then began to spin as it elegantly floated down, landing on Nessa, who picked it up and tossed it again.

"Twenty-four hours," said Caius to no one in particular.

"And we still have to retake Alceron before the Gronch arrive," said Silas.

The deep ringing alarm interrupted them. "Attention please! This is an official announcement. There has been a meteor strike in sector fourteen, no casualties reported. Announcement ends."

Rastus picked up the piece of paper and tossed it into the air again.

"Cheer up, you lot," said Breckin, entering the room. "We haven't lost yet. In fact, things are looking rather bright with Andrade alive and Jaros to arrive in a few hours."

"But the odds are still a bit long," said Caius.

"Don't you believe it. I've known Calron for a good many years now and I'm prepared to bet he's got something planned. I wouldn't be surprised if that thing on the bench out there is going to win the battle for us, even if he does deny it."

Tap, tap, tap.

"What was that?" asked Kayla.

Tap, tap, tap.

"I don't know; it seems to be coming from the secret door," said Breckin.

"Could someone have found it?" asked Silas.

"You girls stay here. We'll go look," said Breckin.

The girls ignored him and followed closely behind. They all crept down the dark passage that led to the hinged panel.

Tap, tap, tap.

"It's louder," whispered Rastus.

Breckin put his hand on the lever that opened the panel. "Okay, stand back."

Kayla watched the panel edge open to reveal a spherical object hovering in the corridor. "What is it?" she whispered.

"It's alien," said Silas. "We don't have anything that looks like that."

Kayla edged a little closer to get a good look. It was round, about six feet across and two feet high.

"Hello," said Breckin. "Do you speak English?"

It ignored him for a second and then started to move slowly forward. When it reached the panel, the disk rolled until it was vertical, allowing it fit through the opening. It then continued on past everyone.

Kayla followed it with the others through the first room and out into the second where Calron was still bending over his device. The disk rotated back to the horizontal as soon as it was through the second doorway.

"Look out, it's going to fire!" shouted Elan.

"I hardly think that's likely," said Calron.

A small opening appeared in the ship and something about six inches tall floated out to land on Calron's hand.

Everyone crowded closer to examine it, being careful not to touch the vehicle, which was still hovering in mid-air.

The small object reminded Kayla of the futuristic toys that were popular when she was young. The object on Calron's hand was motionless.

"What is it?" whispered Nessa.

"He is Ralno of Taador," replied Calron.

"Is it—I mean he—alive?"

"Very much so, and apparently rather excited at having contacted us."

"He doesn't look very excited," said Caius.

A tiny high-pitched voice came from the small metallic creature. "Oh but we are! The battle against the Gronch was nearly over. Our forces were spent, when suddenly half the Gronch battle fleet withdrew. We set out to discover the reason for this and have succeeded!"

Silas stifled a laugh. "You are the aliens the Gronch are at war with?" he asked.

The tiny creature floated over to Silas and stopped, just a few inches in front of his nose. "You find something humorous in that?" it asked.

"No, not at all."

"You don't, for instance, think that we are a little small?"

"No, nothing of the sort. What does size mean?"

The tiny creature paused dangerously and then said, "That's odd, we thought you were ridiculously large!" and burst out laughing, shaking like a thimble on steroids.

When it had recovered from what it clearly thought was a tremendously funny joke, it continued, "In fact, we had a good deal of trouble finding you at all. We normally associate carbon-based creatures with the lower forms of life. At first, we thought you were just some kind of mobile mould."

"Huh!" said Rastus.

"No offence implied. Anyway, we questioned your comps but they are only barely sentient and not designed for communicating with aliens. Fortunately, they were bright enough to direct us to Calron, who has kindly explained the situation and also helped us with your language. By the way, I've been asked to apologize for the hole in your planetoid. We didn't realize the gas inside was of a life-giving nature. I trust no one was hurt?"

"None have been reported and the repair crew would have had it fixed in minutes," said Andrade. "Anyway, Alceron is designed to survive a few small holes."

Nessa absentmindedly tossed the paper spinner into the air again. Ralno immediately zipped over and followed it down to the ground, saying, "How does it fly? I cannot detect a propulsion unit!"

"It floats on the air," explained Caius.

"Oh, the stuff you breathe," said the tiny voice. "Will you throw it again, please?"

Nessa picked it up and tossed it into the air. This time the tiny creature zipped underneath it and grabbed hold. "Weeeeeeee," he yelled, as the paper plummeted downwards with his added weight.

A second tiny creature emerged from the saucer and hovered over to watch. In a moment they were joined by several more.

No one noticed when soon after Andrade had whispered in a few ears and several people had slipped out of the room, the air was still full of tiny creatures hurtling about on various odd shaped pieces of paper.

"Weeeeee!" *Splat.*

"This is Jaros. Requesting clearance to dock."

"Very funny. Now give us your real ID or get off the air!"

Jaros hit the visual switch. "Say again?"

"I said get, ah, oh, sir, sorry. We thought you were missing."

"I was, but now I'm found. Are you going to tell me where to park this thing?"

"What sort of ship, sir?"

"Gronch scout ship."

After a short pause: "That's not on our list. You'd better come in to bay twenty-three. We can take most anything there."

"Thanks, out."

"Out."

Jowett beeped disapprovingly. "Did you have to announce our arrival like that? Now Ranic will be waiting for us."

"If I hadn't, they would have blown us out of space. We are in an enemy ship!"

"What about our large green friend here? You didn't mention him. How do you plan to smuggle in four hundred pounds of alien?"

"Smuggle! I wouldn't dream of it. I'm the Prince. I don't have to pussyfoot around."

"You are communicating with the robot again?" asked Grumm.

"Yes."

"Via tiny vibrations in the air?"

"Yep, you've got it."

"And when the vibrations from the robot reach the flaps on the side of your head, they suddenly turn into thoughts?"

"Yes, more or less."

Grumm watched Jaros for a long moment. *"You wouldn't lie to me, would you?"*

"No!"

"At least telepathy is understandable. A thought leaves one mind and enters another: simple. But this thing you call talking is a little farfetched."

"Honest, it's as real as you or me."

The ship lurched, forcing Jaros to grab hold of a handrail.

"We are docked, sir," said Jowett.

"A bit rough?"

"I'm sorry, sir. The Gronch controls do not allow for finesse."

Jaros peered cautiously out into the hanger deck. *"It looks clear. Stick close to me."*

They hadn't taken more than a few steps before half a dozen security guards intercepted them.

"Don't move."

"Do you know who you're speaking too?" demanded Jaros in his most officious voice.

"Are these creatures stopping us?" asked Grumm.

"Yes."

"I'm speaking to the bloke who came out of an enemy ship with an enemy alien not two feet behind him."

"Would you like me to squash them?"

"No! Not yet, anyway. I think I can deal with them."

"I'm Jaros, Crown Prince. Maybe you've heard of me?"

The guard leaned closer and peered at Jaros' face. "Oh, ah."

Just then two men dressed in the black uniform of the palace guard appeared. "We'll take over here. You can go back to what you were doing."

The hanger guard was still a little shaken, but this was at least something he could deal with. The palace guards were always trying to take over the place. "I'm afraid this is outside your jurisdiction," he said.

The shorter of the two palace guard officers produced a small card. "We have an authorization."

"Oh bother!" thought the hanger guard as he checked the card through his scanner. "Okay. They're all yours," he said.

"Have the lot of you gone crazy?" exclaimed Jaros. "I'm the Crown Prince! You can't pass me around like a can of dog meat!"

The hanger guard shrugged his shoulders and pointed to the authorization card. "Orders are orders, sir." He left with his men, apparently satisfied that he had given an ample explanation.

"If you'll come this way, sir," encouraged one of the guards.

Jaros wasn't used to being ignored. He didn't deal with it very well. "I'm not coming anywhere with anyone. *I'm* the Prince. I give *you* the orders, have you got that?"

"Yes, of course you do. Just down this passageway," said the guard, guiding Jaros around another corner.

"And when I give orders people jump, do you hear me?"

"Yes, sir."

"Funny, I don't recognize either of you. I know most of the palace staff quite well. Are you new?"

"Yes, sir. Just employed today, actually."

"Really. Maybe that explains it. In the future you're both going to have to buck up your—huh?" Jaros stopped in mid-sentence. They had just entered a small room.

On the floor were four bodies, two stripped to their undergarments. Standing in the middle of the room were two men. Jaros choked, "Dad?"

"In the flesh," replied Andrade.

"You're alive!"

"And so are you, thanks to the fact that we intercepted your reception committee."

"Ranic?"

"Yes," said Andrade. "He's definitely getting out of hand. It's about time you did something about him."

"Me?"

"I may be alive, but I'm not running things anymore. One of the reasons I continued to play dead was to give you a good run at the helm. This is your mess; you fix it!"

"Right, then," replied Jaros. "No time like the present."

"Come with me, Grumm. We're going to effect a coup."

Jaros marched confidently down the corridor followed by the two guard officers, Grumm, Jowett, Andrade, and Breckin. Taking absolutely no care at all, Jaros traipsed right through the busiest passageways. With a prince, a dead king, and a giant alien, most people who saw them couldn't decide what to be most surprised at.

"So who are you two?" asked Jaros.

"Caius," said Caius.

"And Silas," said Silas.

"Your future brothers-in-law," explained Caius.

"And I think we should point out that we are under strict orders to keep you alive until the happy event can take place. Until then, we'd be very grateful if you could avoid attempting any dangerously heroic actions."

"I promise to try to stay alive, much as it goes against the grain."

A siren screamed into life. The sound, which had signalled the beginning of every new day for as long as anyone could remember, was finally being used for its real purpose. Everyone froze in their tracks and stared up at the public vid screens coming online. "We regret to announce that a fleet of Gronch destroyers has been detected approaching Alceron. Please report to emergency stations."

"Hurry up," said Jaros, as he started jogging along. "We're running out of time."

Idonea studied her image in her mirror and freshened her makeup. She was determined to look her best while directing the fleet.

"Father?"

Ranic looked up from his desk. "Yes, dear?"

Idonea's cold eyes stared past his face, prodding at his mental defences. "What are you up to, father? Are you going to get us all killed?"

"I shouldn't think so."

She wasn't convinced. She folded her arms and waited.

"Don't worry, dear. Everything will be fine. You'd better get to the control room very soon."

"Ok. But don't think I trust you. I know you better than anyone. I know when you are plotting something big. I'm going to be mighty cross if I end up dead at the end of this!" With a final contemptuous flick of her head, she turned and stormed off.

Ranic shook his head as the door slid shut after her. He knew perfectly well she would lose; their puny defence force wouldn't last more than five minutes. It really didn't matter who controlled the fleet, but if his plans all worked out as intended, she would be fine. He may not like her much, but family was family. Now, if only his peace treaty succeeded.

The coming surprise attack made the problem a little more urgent, but Ranic was still confident that any sufficiently advanced society would be able to understand profit, or bribery at the very least.

First he had to deal with the idiotic council. With all the difficult members safely locked up, Ranic was quietly confident. He entered the council chamber to confront them. As Ranic took his place, the chairs of the absent councillors appeared to glare angrily at him. The handful of members actually present did the same.

"We have called you to this meeting as there have been widespread reports of what can only be described as treasonous acts. Hundreds of people have disappeared, and the palace guard are implicated in most of the abductions. Add to this, almost forty percent of the reservists have failed to report to their assigned areas."

Ranic was a little stunned. He hadn't expected an attack from the remnants of the council. Still, he knew how to deal with committees. "I'm well aware of these events and don't think for a moment that the culprit is going to get away unpunished. I already have good information that the culprit is now in this very room!"

Ranic let his mental shield drop just enough during his last sentence to allow the councillors to see he was telling the truth. The previously united councillors peered at one another with ominous mistrust.

Heindmarsh, a young councillor, spoke up. "What about the prince? Is the rumour that he was lost to a Gronch ship true?"

"I'm afraid so," confirmed Ranic. "There is little hope of him rescuing us at this point. Much as we'd all love to see him bound in through that door, I fear we are going to have to face this trial alone."

One of the older councillors shrugged and shook his head slowly, "We are lost. The Gronch will make short work of us. It has all been for naught!"

"I fear you may be right," agreed Ranic. "Without a strong leader during the next few hours we are almost certainly lost. If only there was someone else who could step in…"

Another councillor spoke up. "What about you, Ranic? We could announce that you've agreed to take power during the crisis!"

"Me?" exclaimed Ranic with mock surprise. "I don't know if I could do that." Then he asked, "Couldn't someone else do it?" Ranic stared coldly around the room, his eyes daring any of them to cross him. "I guess I'll have to then, but, only while the emergency lasts," he concluded modestly.

Ranic could see that a good number of the more sensible councillors were looking rather cross. They had come all fired up to argue about other things and were just now realizing what had just been decided in their presence.

"Hang on," started one of them.

Ranic quickly interrupted, "The immediate problem is to defend Alceron. I suggest we defer any further discussion until a later date."

Muffled shouts could be heard from outside the council chamber, followed by a scream. The double doors of the chamber burst open. Through the door, Ranic could see two guards dangling upside down, their legs held by the claws of a gigantic green monster. The receptionist was sprawled across the floor, a palace guard attempting to revive her. The Prince stood in the middle of the open doors.

"Is this a council meeting? Sorry I'm a bit late, but I was being held prisoner on a Gronch battle cruiser."

"You're alive!" exclaimed Heindmarsh.

Ranic recovered from his initial shock. "It does my heart good to see you again, Jaros. We thought you were lost for certain. What an uncanny ability you have to escape death." He pointed towards Grumm. "Are we to infer that you have become acquainted with one of our enemies?"

"You certainly may infer that. This is Grumm," Jaros waved to Grumm to put the guards down and come forward. "He helped me escape."

Heindmarsh said, "Then we owe him a debt of thanks for returning our leader in the nick of time."

"If that's what actually happened," put in Ranic.

"What do you mean?"

"Don't you think it a little strange? I mean, has anyone ever heard of a Gronch defecting before?"

Jaros smiled. "You think he might be a double agent or somehow controlling me?"

"Anything's possible. We don't know what the Gronch may be capable of. It's even possible that they brainwashed you!"

"Don't tell me that you think that I should be placed under house arrest as a safety measure, just until the hostilities are over?"

"I think it would be best," replied Ranic.

"Yes, I think I can see exactly what you mean," Jaros said. "Guards, arrest this man."

Caius and Silas leapt to either side of Ranic and took hold of him.

"What!" exclaimed Ranic, struggling ineffectively. "You can't arrest me!"

"Yes, I can, and I just have."

Ranic was furious. "He's mad. Release me at once. Being held captive has warped his mind."

"Far from it." Jaros turned to one of the other councillors, "Langton, if you take a couple of squads into the palace dungeons, I think you'll find our missing councillors and others who have recently disappeared. Meanwhile, the rest of you had better get back to work. We've got a war to win!"

Ranic muttered sadly to himself as Silas and Caius dragged him out of the council chamber. "So close..."

Caius laughed. "I expect you might have just managed it, too, if the so-called list of people most likely to take your side, which you got from the city comp, hadn't been fabricated."

"What!"

Caius continued. "But, after being locked up for a few days and tortured, I expect most of them will have had a change of heart."

CHAPTER EIGHTEEN

I donea reclined in the controller's chair. The first attack would begin soon. She felt for the mind of each pilot, giving orders to several who were not yet in formation.

The control room was crowded. Several VIPs had pushed their way in, as well as the usual complement of officers who actually had a reason for being there. Idonea didn't mind; she liked being watched, although for the first time in her life she was not entirely certain what would happen.

Idonea was surprised to see the door slide open and a small crowd of people march in. At the front was Kayla — that damn Earth girl again. Who the hell let her in? Oh, cripes, Jaros was with her!

Kayla returned Idonea's malevolent look and waited for Jaros to speak. He paused for a couple of seconds while the whispers died down.

"My, my, my! Haven't we got a lot of new bridge personnel?"

Several dignitaries tried unsuccessfully to melt into the walls.

"I'd like to thank you all for carrying on so well in my absence."

Idonea looked distraught. "That's okay. I'm happy to continue."

"No, I wouldn't dream of it. Kayla, here, will be taking over."

Kayla's eyes popped open. "Me?"

"Yes, you."

"She can't do it," insisted Idonea vehemently. "I've been in training all my life. You can't entrust our lives to an untrained Earth girl!"

"I can and I will. Now, if you wouldn't mind leaving," Jaros gestured towards the door. "We don't have time to chat just at the moment."

"I'm not going!"

"Grumm, would you mind?"

"I would enjoy it," thought Grumm. He happily trundled over to the bridge and picked up Idonea by the ankles. He considered that the correct way to pick up a human. He then carried her out utterly oblivious to her screams of protest.

Jaros scanned the faces still present. "If the other non-essential personnel wouldn't mind leaving, then we can get on with it."

No one else needed to be told twice. There was a mad rush for the door.

"Good," said Jaros when the room was empty of spectators. "Status report, please."

"Two divisions currently deployed, sir. Another is standing by. All Alceron spheres report they are battle ready. Scouts are reporting movement from the Gronch fleet."

Jaros gestured toward the controller's chair. "Kayla, you'd better get ready."

"You're not serious, are you? You can do it much better than I."

"I'm afraid not. I may know the strategy backward and forward, but I've never handled more than fifteen at once; but fifteen against the Gronch fleet of hundreds won't do us much good. You can keep in contact with every ship we have."

"But what good is that, if I don't know what to tell them all to do?"

"You won't have to. I'll be making the decisions. You just have to pass on my commands and protect the pilots against MT attacks."

"Is that all?" muttered Kayla to herself before grudgingly sitting down at the controller's station.

A commotion sounded outside and the door slid open. Rastus slipped past the guard whom Jaros had left just outside and stood catching his breath.

"What's happened?" Jaros asked.

"It's the Silinians. They left about three minutes ago. One moment I was chatting to one of them, and the next they had all disappeared into their ship and took off down the corridor at top speed. Calron says he can't detect them anywhere."

"Drat," said Jaros, "I was hoping they might be of some help. Never mind, we'll just have to manage." He sat down next to Kayla and closed his eyes to concentrate.

"Here they come. What should I do?" asked Kayla.

"Wait a second... Ok. Now bring that section down and forward."

Kayla channelled the instructions to fifteen of the Alceron ships and watched as they swooped downwards.

"Now send those seven straight up and those two over there."

"Where?"

"There. Are you still blocking them all?"

"Yes."

"Tell those three to start firing in two seconds and those down there, tell them to move up."

"Them?"

"No, them!"

"Sorry. Oh, stuff it, we're getting attacked over there."

"Send those three in, and order all to pull back."

Elan tried to watch as much as she could, but spent most of her time searching through space trying to find someone. And then, to build up a picture she had to remember each person she found and then look for the next. Even the little she could see made it clear things were not going well. There were too many Gronch ships and they kept ganging up.

To trap an inertia-less ship, you needed to surround it with at least four ships to stop it from escaping. Elan could see how Jaros kept trying to surround one of the enemy ships but with every attempt had to keep pulling back to defend his own.

The door to the control room slid open again and Calron walked in. He moved quietly to Elan's side in order not to disturb Kayla or Jaros and whispered, "How is it going?"

"Not too well."

"Have we lost any ships?"

"Not yet, but Jaros can't keep squirming our ships out of trouble much longer. We're going to run out of luck soon."

"I wouldn't bet on it," said Calron, mysteriously.

"What do you mean?"

"Look out in that direction, as far as you can," said Calron, casually indicating a direction in space.

Elan searched outwards past the Gronch ships. "I can't find anything."

"Are you sure?" asked Calron, sounding a little worried.

"Nothing... wait a minute, yes! There's a ship there, coming this way fast. Hang on, there's more coming. Holy smokes!"

"I take it from your expletive that the reinforcements are on time?"

Kayla was getting tired. Jaros' commands were coming faster as he continued to foil the Gronch attacks.

"Hi sis. Sorry we're a bit late. Can you use another thousand ships?"

"Shhh! I'm busy." Kayla couldn't help from smiling, but now she was in real trouble; there were too many ships. Jaros was rattling instructions but she couldn't keep up. He had to keep repeating himself.

A broad, hideous smile broke over Graator's leathery green face, revealing his less-than-pearly-white fangs. He surveyed the approaching reinforcements, savouring the anticipation of destroying them.

If only their ships didn't keep backing off whenever he got them cornered. Whoever was controlling these primitives was taking undue measures to ensure that none of them were lost, as if each one was important in some way. Graator manoeuvred another attack into position, aiming at capturing a single ship, but again his enemy broke off and simply concentrated on retrieving that single ship. It was crazy. Not only were they spending all their time on defence, but also half the primitives' ships simply drifted around with no clear purpose at all. Several times, Graator had almost succeeded in surrounding an entire group when they suddenly retreated. What could be the point in delaying such simple manoeuvres to the last moment?

Finally, a rare and frightening thought awakened deep inside Graator's evil mind. A more insidious and dangerous process, curiosity, briefly overpowered his lust for destruction! Following the thin threads of thought through space, he traced them back to his adversary and received an almost fatal shock — it was nothing but a human female! Impossible!

He tried again, being more careful and again reached the same conclusion. This time he lingered, observing her mind at work. She seemed to be struggling, as if distracted by something. Graator watched silently, picking up on any stray thought, being careful not to trigger her defences.

She was definitely being distracted by something other than the battle. Finally he saw a pattern; every few seconds the female would send a fleetingly brief thought and always to the same place. Graator traced it to a small ship, which seemed just outside the theatre of action. Experimentally he sent a single ship out toward it. The female reacted instantly by bringing other ships over to protect it. Leaning back, Graator contemplated how best to make use of his little discovery.

"Here they come, Jaros. They mean business this time!"

Jaros was worried. Kayla would lose it if he went any faster; but if he slowed down, they were going to start losing men.

Kayla was flat out, defending the heaviest attack the Gronch had attempted. They seemed to be attacking everywhere at once. The link to Jaros was getting faster, but it still wasn't smooth enough for this kind of manoeuvring. If they'd had a few weeks to practice, it might have been possible.

A split second too late Kayla suddenly clicked to what the Gronch were up to! *"They've trapped Mark! What should I do?"*

Jaros was silent for almost a full second before he replied in slow deliberate thoughts, *"Nothing. We've lost him. They've got six ships around him and we haven't got anything near enough."*

Kayla was stunned. *"But!"* She watched as the shields of Mark's ship weakened rapidly. His ship was under heavy fire from the Gronch. Jaros was sending to her, but she wasn't listening.

"Snap out of it, Kayla!" shouted Jaros aloud, shaking her. *"We can't stop or others will die, too."*

"You take over."

"I can't."

"Garbage! I kept feeling you starting to take over, but you pulled back each time. Just try, damn it! I can see what you're capable of, even if you can't!"

Thoughts flashed through Jaros' head. Could he really do it? In all his life he'd never controlled more than ten or twelve pieces in a Stragaw game. He knew the strategy, but mentally keeping in contact with all of them and shielding them from the Gronch the way Kayla had been doing gave him pause.

He looked over to Kayla, intending to convince her to try again, but the look on her face stopped him dead. She thought he could do it; she really believed it! What the hell?

Even the few fractions of a second spent in indecision might have been too long. Mark's ship was definitely lost, but most of the others being attacked could possibly be saved. Jaros started to take control of the ships in immediate danger, slowly at first, still conscious of each extra ship, expecting to run into his limit any second. The effort to rescue as many ships as possible consumed him. He brought in more and more ships, planning by instinct, with no time to worry about how he was doing it. His mind seemed to be spreading out endlessly.

Kayla didn't wait to see if Jaros would manage it. She knew perfectly well he could. She had something more important on her mind.

"Energy down to twenty percent. The shields will go in a few more seconds."

Alex thumped the side of the vid screen. "Where the heck are they? If those ships were firing at us full power, we'd have disintegrated by now."

"They might not be coming. We've no way of knowing how far away the rest of our other ships are."

Alex tried to search out through space with his mind, but only managed to find Mark, who was, after all, only three feet away. "Damn! I wish we'd had more time to practice with this MT stuff. You'd think they could have let us in on this a bit sooner."

"You know they couldn't. Anyway, we can receive instructions okay and that's all we need." Another warning beeper interrupted Mark as their shields began to collapse.

"Why don't you check with your sister?" suggested Alex.

"I can't. Interrupting her could cost someone's life."

"What about that friend of hers? Do you think you could find her?"

"Don't know, I've only spoken to her through Kayla. I guess I could try."

"Get on with it then."

"Elan?" Mark waited expectantly, and then tried again. *"Elan?"*

"Is that you, Mark?"

"Yes. Sorry to bother you, but we're about to get fried here. Any chance of a last minute reprieve?"

"I'm not sure. You're cut off from the rest of our ships. It doesn't look good."

"Oh—I guess this is goodbye then."

"Not bloody likely! Kayla promised me a date with you and mortality isn't going to get you out of it!"

Mark couldn't help smiling. *"Well, I wouldn't want to break a promise."*

"That's more like it."

Mark decided to use his last-resort emergency tactic. "Come on Alex, think of something clever, quickly!"

"Why?"

"Because I've got a date and I don't want to miss it!"

"We're on a ship, in deep space, about to be fried alive, and you've been arranging yourself a date?"

"No time like the present. That's what you always say."

Alex was speechless; then he came back to his senses. "Has she got a friend?"

"Elan, I'm afraid I can't make it unless you've got a friend for my buddy here."

Elan was stumped for a second. Then she spotted Nessa lurking in the corner. *"Would he mind if she was a little young?"*

"I don't think so," replied Mark and then said to Alex, "Okay, I've got you a date, now think of something."

"Ummmm."

Suddenly their ship lurched sideways. At first Mark thought it was the shield collapsing, but then he saw the vid screen — one after another, each of the ships surrounding them either flared into brilliant incandescence or disintegrated into hundreds of tiny pieces.

Alex picked himself off the floor and grinned maniacally, "Good, wasn't it?"

"What did you do?"

Alex grinned. "I don't think I'm going to tell you."

Slowly Mark realized, "So let me guess; your brilliant plan was to have all the enemy ships suddenly blow themselves to bits for no apparent reason?"

"Well, it worked, didn't it?" laughed Alex, and then examined his reflection in one of the panels on his control board. "Anyway, the important thing is that we've both got dates!"

Kayla took a deep breath and wiped the perspiration from her face. She had exhausted herself pulling the first three ships apart before it occurred to her that a well-placed bend in one of the weapons tubes would achieve the same goal. She was about to start looking for some more targets when the doors to the bridge slid open. The unfortunate guards were pushed aside by the Silinian's spacecraft and one of the aliens emerged from the ship to hover near Calron's head.

"Greetings water bags—whoops!" said Rompith in his tiny metallic voice. "I mean, greetings, humans. I'm pleased to be able to tell you that the mighty Silinian fleet is at this very moment joining you in battle."

Kayla quickly scanned the battle to try and spot the new ships but couldn't detect a thing. "Are you sure? I can't sense them."

"You forget, perhaps, that we are not telepathic, and therefore not capable of being detected by your MT abilities."

"Then how do your ships know which way to go?" asked Elan.

"Guesswork mostly. Our ships fly around at random until they happen to pass within detector range of an enemy ship. They send out a signal to alert other Silinian ships. If enough happen to be within a few light-seconds of the adversary, they converge and attack.

"That's what we normally do, anyway; but with your ships to follow we will be able to do considerably more damage than usual. Remember, the Gronch commander cannot sense our ships, so he will not know if he is outnumbered in any given area."

"Which means he will wait too long before reacting to apparently pointless attacks!" exclaimed Elan.

"That is the idea, yes."

Graator bellowed another obscenity and spat in the general direction of the human fleet. His incompetent pilots were somehow managing to lose their ships. On the bright side, they were getting themselves killed in the process, saving him the chore.

One of his newer advisors bravely spoke up, *"Sir, we are losing too many ships. Wouldn't a tactical withdrawal be advisable?"*

"Is it your view that our mighty Gronch fleet, under my personal command, is losing to a bunch of primitives, and that this being the case we should turn tail and run?"

"Umm, no sir, not at all. I was just thinking that we might want to regroup, to give ourselves a chance to iron out whatever the current problem is, before wiping out these nasty little creatures." Graator paused for a few dangerous moments. *"Your suggestion is not altogether without merit. However, the Gronch never retreat!"*

The young officer was about to respond, when a couple of the older advisors took pity on their younger colleague and quickly hustled him into a back room before he could shorten his life expectancy further.

"Yes!" shouted Nessa when several Gronch ships disappeared at once.

Elan elbowed her. "Shhh."

Nessa whispered back, "But we're slaughtering them. They're going down like a pack of cards now."

"We may be wiping out their ships, but that still leaves their battle cruisers."

Nessa turned her mind back to the battle, which seemed to be rapidly coming to an end as Gronch ships disappeared every couple of seconds. Finally, a sense of self-preservation seemed to return and the last remaining Gronch ships crowded back to the safety of the gigantic battle cruisers.

Jaros considered the problem for several seconds. He opened his eyes and looked around the room. "Any suggestions?" he asked. "Those cruisers have too much firepower for our ships. If we attack, they will just pick us off one at a time with their big guns. It looks like a stalemate."

Calron pretended to clear his electronic throat. "Ahem."

"Yes?"

"Can I draw your attention to that blank section of wall?" said Calron, pointing.

Everyone watched it expectantly. Suddenly, the entire panel slid open and a pilot's console emerged from the wall.

"Alceron spheres don't have inertia less drives and ship-to-ship blasters!" pointed out one of the officers.

"Of course they do," replied Calron. "What do you think I designed them for? They are bigger, faster, and have more firepower than the Gronch cruisers."

The gears turned slowly within Jaros' mind for a couple of seconds before he got the idea. He looked quickly around the room, fixed his eyes on Silas and said, "Well hurry up then; we aren't going to fly anywhere without a pilot."

Silas stepped sideways and looked behind himself to find the person Jaros was talking to. Finding nothing but a wall, he suddenly understood and quickly walked over and took the pilots station.

Jaros straightened out the chaos on the other six Alceron bridges and soon had all seven spheres heading towards the nearest Gronch battle cruiser. Kayla gripped Jaros for support when the whole planetoid began to shake with blasts from the Gronch cruiser. The powerful Gronch shields held for several minutes, but with seven against one, they couldn't last forever.

The Gronch shields finally buckled. The gigantic Alceron blasters ripped the cruiser into subatomic particles in a fraction of a second, leaving nothing more substantial than an occasional gaseous molecule drifting harmlessly in space.

CHAPTER NINETEEN

*E*lan paced back and forth, waiting for Mark to emerge from one of the air locks.

Nessa asked, "How many battle cruisers are left now?"

After a brief pause Elan replied, "Three. It's taking longer to catch up with each one, but they can't get out of range. Another three or four hours should finish it."

"Is that him?" asked Nessa, pointing to a young man emerging from a distant air lock.

"No, I think Mark's taller—according to Kayla's description. There he is!" exclaimed Elan.

"Hmmm, cute!" said Nessa.

"He's mine, hands off."

"I was only looking! Anyway, who's that with him?"

"I think that must be Alex."

"Oh, goody!"

Mark stood in the enormous hanger with a dazed look on his face. Elan appeared through the crowd, reached up, and kissed him.

"Hi," said Mark. "What was that for?"

Before Elan could think of anything to say, Nessa cut in. "It's the custom here for all returning heroes."

Then, taking advantage of her own fib, she followed Elan's fine example and kissed Alex.

Alex sent a thought over to Mark: *"I think I'm going to like it here."* He then asked Nessa, "Do you think you could show me where I can get this leg of mine looked at? I took a bit of a fall and I think it may need strapping."

Nessa looked towards Elan.

"Go on."

"The hospital is just a couple of sections over," said Nessa, adding, "Lean on me if you like."

"Thanks."

Elan watched silently as Nessa and Alex disappeared into the crowd, wishing for a moment that she had the nerve to use a trick like that. Instead, she just stood there staring at Mark.

"Is there somewhere I can get cleaned up? We've been stuck on our ships for a few days."

"Follow me."

Mark stuck close to her while they were weaving through the crowded hanger. It was strange to meet a girl in the flesh after speaking to her telepathically. She seemed like an old friend somehow, and although he hadn't formed a mental picture of her, he knew who she was the second he saw her.

There was a slightly awkward silence as they made their way along the passages. Mark realized that neither of them really knew what their relationship was. They came to an elevator and had to wait for it to arrive. Elan asked, "How is it that all of your pilots happened to be MT latent?"

"Apparently, someone from here was screening the space patrol applicants and only latent telepaths were accepted. Same as someone from here must have designed our ships; the inertia-less drives just needed to be activated."

The lift doors opened and they crowded in with about ten other people. "Sounds like more of Calron's handiwork."

They were both stuck in the back corner of the lift. Mark felt his hand accidentally touch Elan's. She didn't move hers away so he let the touch continue, holding his breath for a brief moment until he felt her fingers close around his.

"Calron's the robot?" said Mark as casually as possible as they stepped out of the lift.

"Yep. He'll probably be the only one in."

Turning down a dead end, Elan led Mark through the wall panel and into their hideout.

Calron lifted his head from the oddly constructed machine that he was working on. "Mark, good to see you made it."

Mark's eyes lit up at the sight of something mechanical. "Do you need a hand? What is it?"

Elan saw the look in Mark's eye and quickly took his hand again to drag him past the lure of boy talk with the robot. "You can play with Calron later. I thought you wanted to get cleaned up."

"Awww," complained Mark as Elan pushed him into the bathroom.

"None of your moaning. Kayla warned me not to take any lip from you. Anyway, Calron has been working on that contraption for weeks and he still hasn't told anyone what it is."

"Okay, okay," said Mark, turning quickly and wrapping his arms around Elan while she was still pushing forward. "Join me?"

Elan struggled half-heartedly to get free, then kissed him quickly before jumping backwards and closing the door before he could grab her again. "You'd be lucky. And don't come out of there until all the grime has dissolved! I'll leave some clean clothes by the door."

"Yes, boss."

"That's better."

Strolling back to the lounge, Elan tried to wipe the grin off her face. She was unsuccessful.

Silas bounded into the lounge with Caius close behind and demanded, "Where is she?"

Elan ignored his question. "I thought you were piloting still?"

"Jaros rotated the bridge staff. Now, quick, we just heard through the MT grapevine that some slimy character is taking liberties with Nessa!"

Caius added, "We can't contact her. Can you scan for her?"

"I could, but I won't."

Silas's mouth dropped open. Caius asked, "Why not?"

"Because if she was in trouble, she'd call for help. Since she hasn't called, she probably doesn't want a couple of great big oafs blundering in and embarrassing her."

"But," started Silas. "But, she's too young."

"Rubbish! She's sixteen; in some cultures that's old maid territory. Anyway, I think you're both jumping to conclusions. You know how the MT gossip gets exaggerated."

Calron, quietly working away at his bench, suddenly rotated his head halfway round in order to address them. "Excuse me, but would anyone be interested in the fact that Nessa and a young man have just turned down the passage towards our door?"

Silas and Caius looked at Calron, then at Elan, then at each other. Caius dived onto a chair. Silas skidded past him, scooped up a magazine that was lying on the floor and landed on the couch just in time to look up and nod nonchalantly as Nessa and Alex entered the room.

"Oh, good, I didn't think anyone would be here. Alex, these are two of my brothers, Silas and Caius."

"Hi," said Alex.

"Look after Alex, will you? I have to go and change before we can go out. I'll be back in a couple of minutes," said Nessa, disappearing into one of the back rooms.

"Have a seat," offered Caius.

"Thanks."

Alex relaxed into the chair. The two brothers seemed to be looking at him in a rather odd way. In fact, their expressions were something less than open and friendly.

"Anyone for a drink?" asked Elan.

Alex waited for one of the brothers to reply, but they seemed to be waiting for him. "Umm, yes, thanks."

"Silas, Caius?" persisted Elan.

They both grunted assent.

"Do you need a hand?" asked Alex hopefully.

"No, I can manage."

"Are you sure?" pleaded Alex.

At last Elan caught on. "Oh, yeah, if you could wash up a mug or two."

"Great," said Alex, jumping up quickly.

"I just need one more."

After a couple of unsuccessful attempts, Alex had to ask Elan to show him how to make the sink work.

She pushed him out of the way. "Don't feel bad — no one can make it work." Then she leaned close and whispered, "They aren't always like this. They will warm up once they get to know you a bit."

Mark wandered in looking very relaxed. "Hi, Alex. How's your leg?"

"Much better."

Alex dragged Mark over to the corner of the kitchen and whispered, "Hey, can you get me out of that blind date? I feel bad about it, but Nessa and I are getting along really well and I couldn't possibly go out with someone else now."

"I don't know. It's a bit rude. I'll check with Elan."

Mark walked over, leaned close to Elan and whispered, "Alex says he wants to cancel that blind date. Is that okay?"

Elan looked very confused and asked loudly, "Why doesn't he want to go out with Nessa?"

Before Mark could say anything Caius and Silas had appeared from nowhere and pinned Alex to the wall.

Silas demanded, "What's wrong with our sister, huh?"

"I don't know what it's like where you come from, but don't think you can toy with a girl's affections and get away with it up here!" said Caius.

"Not bloody likely," agreed Silas.

Mark, who had just figured it out, stood back and watched, trying desperately not to laugh.

"Now, are you going to take her out or are we going to have to get physical?" asked Caius menacingly.

"She's the one I want to take out," said Alex, still sounding very confused.

Silas smiled. "That's the idea; but you'd better be more convincing in front of Nessa."

Elan was about to protest that they couldn't make him take her out, but Mark quickly hustled her out into the lounge and explained what had happened.

"Shouldn't I explain to Caius and Silas?" she whispered.

"Sure," agreed Mark, with a mischievous grin. "But you've got to let me enjoy the moment for a while. It's nice to see him in the soup by himself for a change. Let's go for a little walk; with luck he'll have gotten himself deeper in trouble by the time we get back."

Jaros stumbled into the passage, leaning heavily on Kayla, who wasn't much better off. "We won," breathed Jaros.

The public vid communicators blared out the good news to all, while Jaros and Kayla passed unnoticed along the back passages. Kayla tried to get Jaros to slow down. "Why are you in such a hurry? Can't we just sit down and rest for a while? You're worn out."

"I'm not stopping until I've had a chance to strangle Calron."

"Why?"

"For getting me captured by the Gronch and then sending along a loony duplicate to drive me mad, as well."

"How did Calron get you captured?"

"I don't know, but he managed it somehow, the little metallic brat!"

At last, they reached the hideout and stumbled into the lounge. "He's probably at his work bench, through here," said Kayla, leading the way and waving hello to Alex, who seemed to be having a very intense conversation with Caius and Silas.

Jaros was trying to think of an appropriate expletive to hurl at Calron. "Well?" he said loudly, then immediately decided it wasn't quite the word he had been looking for.

Calron, working away rapidly at a console, appeared to be ignoring them but eventually replied without looking up, "Your question allows for a good number of answers. Perhaps you could rephrase it?"

"You know bloody well what I'm talking about. Why did you get me captured?"

Kayla joined in. "He could have been killed. It was only a fluke that he got out alive!"

"I quite agree," said Calron.

Jaros pounced. "So, even you admit it was stupid; and yet, you still did it!"

"Me?" asked Calron innocently.

"It must have been you. Who else could have built a duplicate of you and switched places without anyone noticing?"

"I won't denying taking part, but it certainly wasn't my idea."

Jaros was speechless while he tried to think who else it could have been. "You aren't trying to claim it was Andrade's idea?"

"Heavens no, he'd have more sense."

"Then who?" demanded Jaros.

Still, without pausing in his work, Calron withdrew his left hand from the console, extended it towards Jaros, turned his palm upwards, and uncurled his metallic fingers. In the centre of his palm was a familiar green pill.

"You took a mind block so the Gronch who picked you up wouldn't realize that you were actually a spy." Calron turned to Kayla, "I did my best to convince him not to do it, but humans can be so jolly pig-headed, don't you think?"

"Yes they can," agreed Kayla, and kicked Jaros in the shin.

"What's that for?" complained Jaros, who was feeling a little lost.

"For nearly getting yourself killed. Try it again and I'll get really violent."

Calron continued, "Of course, I wasn't going to risk my own neck on his hair-brained scheme, so, I whipped up a quick duplicate using one of your comps. Did it function okay? I was a bit rushed."

Jaros swallowed the pill, ignored Calron's question and stormed out of the room, muttering something about oversized calculators.

EPILOGUE

S everal weeks later, Mark and Elan were strolling through one of Alceron's main shopping levels.

Elan asked, "Are you sure you don't want to go back with them?"

"Yes."

"I wouldn't mind."

"I would."

"Okay, but don't blame me if you get homesick in a few weeks."

"Look, it's fine. We can both go when you get some leave."

"But don't you want to get back to the patrol?"

"No. I've had enough excitement. I've been thinking about making a career move."

"What did you have in mind?"

"I thought we could open up an MT school back on earth. You can handle the advanced courses. I'll give beginners lessons. There's going to be a real demand for it now. We should be able to make a small fortune."

"You want me to prostitute my talents just to make money?" asked Elan in mock shock.

"Oh, heavens no, now that I think about it, I wouldn't dream of asking you to do such a thing." Mark paused thoughtfully for a second, "How about if we went into franchises, running a whole chain of MT schools? Then we'd make a whopping great big fortune!"

"That sounds better," said Elan and then pointed. "Hey, what's going on there?"

Mark followed her finger to a small shop across the street. It was crowded with people. Across the top of the entrance was a large sign that read, "Gronch stew, best meal in the galaxy. Taste the fruits of victory here!"

"Let's try it," suggested Elan.

"It's probably just someone trying to make money out of the war."

Elan dragged him towards it.

Mark gave in. "All right. Don't pull my arm off!"

They pushed their way in and quickly grabbed a table when another couple got up to leave.

"Where's the menu?" asked Mark.

The double doors bounced open and a familiar looking robot hurried out carrying a tray of plates covered with an odd looking substance. "It's Calron!" exclaimed Elan.

The robot danced between the tables, depositing plates in front of people. When he got to their table he said in a quiet voice: "Jowett's the name, waiting is the game; two standard orders?"

"Yes, I guess so," said Elan.

"Very good, a wise choice, of course. There isn't anything else on the menu. So, that makes it simple, doesn't it?" Then before they could say anything in reply he was racing back towards the kitchen, shouting, "Two more standards, Grumm!"

As soon as the air lock opened, they burst out. It was designed to accommodate two people in spacesuits; but

even without suits, four was a little cramped. Ignoring the
ladder, Nessa jumped the short distance down to the grass.
She called back in delight, "It's soft!"

Alex caught up with her. "Take off your shoes."

She looked at him doubtfully, well aware that she
wasn't exempt from his practical jokes.

"No tricks," said Alex, innocently. "Look, I'll take
mine off, too."

Nessa waited until he had removed both of his
shoes before following suit. She balanced on one foot
and gingerly touched the ground with her toes and then
let her whole foot sink into the grass. "Mmmm," she
murmured, removing her other shoe.

"Like it?" asked Alex.

"Yes, it's quite soothing," she replied.

Alex picked her up and kissed her.

"Where did the others go?" she asked after kissing
him back.

"I think they went to assess the damage. You aren't
bothered by the open skies?"

Nessa looked upwards. "No, should I be? The air
conditioning needs adjusting though and the light is a
bit bright."

"We like to refer to that as a humid breeze and a
sunny day. Wait 'till you get caught in a rainstorm.
Then you'll appreciate how nice this is."

"Oh! I wasn't complaining, just remarking upon it.
One is supposed to, isn't one?"

"Yes, I suppose so. You might need to practice a
bit," said Alex, grinning.

Jaros wandered through the charred remains of
Kayla's house. He wasn't really looking at it; he was
trying to figure out what he might have done to upset
Kayla. She'd seemed rather distant for the last couple of
days. Eventually, he made his way back to where she
was staring morosely at a small pile of rubble. "What's
wrong?" he asked.

"Nothing."

"Bull!"

Kayla pushed the rubble around with the tip of her foot for a few moments. "It's Alfred."

"What about him?"

"He's gone. I lost him when we were picked up. I've asked around but no one seems to know what happened to him."

"We'll get another house comp, Kayla."

"You don't understand."

"Then explain it for me. Please."

"Okay, okay. It's just that Alfred wasn't an ordinary comp. He was more like the parents we never had. He was always there, giving advice, making sure we got to school on time." Kayla smiled.

"What?"

"I was just thinking, you know, when you reach that age when one of the adults takes you aside for a roundabout talk on the facts of life?"

Jaros tried not to laugh. "He didn't!"

"He did, with full colour moving images on the vid screen." She was smiling broadly now.

"You're joking."

Kayla was having trouble getting the words out. "Complete with close-ups of bees pollinating plants."

Jaros burst out laughing with her.

Poking through the remains, Kayla uncovered a barely recognizable lump of metal that once must have been a frying pan. "He couldn't cook, either. He kept claiming that it was due to mechanical failures in the kitchen unit, but I don't think he ever really understood what it was about his cooking that was going wrong." Kayla started to look a little down again. "It won't be the same without him."

Jaros took her hand. "We'd better go. We can't miss the grand unveiling."

When the four of them arrived back in orbit after their short visit to the surface, they found Rastus waiting at the air lock to hurry them along.

"Calron's got everyone else waiting for you. He won't do anything until you get there."

Kayla held Jaros' hand as they entered the common room. Andrade's tall form was leaning against a wall while Breckin paced impatiently. "About time, too! Can we get started now? The ship can't stay on autopilot forever!" Breckin said.

Calron stood next to his machine, which was partly covered by a bed sheet.

"Well, go on, pull it off," encouraged Rastus.

"Not just yet," said Calron. "We have all been through a great deal in the last few weeks, and I think we would all benefit from a review of events, now that the necessity for secrecy is no longer with us."

Alex whispered in Nessa's ear, "Do you get the feeling he's about to announce that the butler did it?"

Calron ignored him, "The story begins nearly sixty years ago, when a small one-man exploration ship passed close enough to the moon I was stranded on to pick up my weak radio transmissions.

"After explaining to the human the danger that his species was in, we began to devise a plan to protect Earth from the Gronch Empire.

"Several things were needed to defeat the Gronch. First, we needed a fleet of at least comparable strength. Technically this was no problem as the Gronch were never very advanced, but it did require a fairly large fleet, and no one on Earth could know about its construction.

"Second, we needed some means to defeat the mental control that the Gronch would certainly use against us. Unfortunately, humans hadn't been using their latent telepathic talents for a very long time, whereas the Gronch live and die by their MT abilities.

"It was possible a breeding program could have produced results given a couple of thousand years, but we couldn't wait that long. Fortunately, since I was constructed I had been considering this very problem, and although unable to generate any MT of my own, I was able to discover some of the basic principles behind it.

"Only a biological brain can generate MT. The only way to combat the Gronch was to create a biological brain with exceptional MT capabilities. It took me fifteen years to understand enough of the human DNA to make the necessary modifications, and even then I was still relying mostly on guesswork. I prepared two embryos — one with a little more emphasis on the MT ability, the other with a little more MK ability."

"Jaros and Kayla," said Rastus.

"Exactly. And to avoid having all our eggs in one basket, Kayla was relocated to Earth as soon as she was old enough."

Surprised, Kayla said, "So that was why Jaros looked familiar when I first met him, and while I was at the orphanage I must have latched on to Mark because he reminded me of Jaros. Although I didn't know it, I was basically searching for my lost bro...?" She stopped dead and exchanged a horrified look with Jaros.

Breckin realized what they were thinking and quickly explained, "No, don't panic; you aren't biologically brother and sister. Calron used completely different sources of DNA."

Calron continued, "Anyway, everything went according to plan until the attempt on Andrade's life. We realized at that point that the society we had designed was becoming too unstable. Another problem had also arisen: Jaros wasn't developing as expected. He seemed to be blocking off most of his abilities.

Apparently he had a deep-seated belief that he couldn't be better than his contemporaries, who were just talented humans, and so he subconsciously limited his own abilities to match theirs."

"We decided that letting Andrade appear to die would avoid any further attempts on his life and leave him free to track down the extent of the instability. Also, we thought that the shock of Andrade's death and the extra responsibility it brought would help Jaros break through his mental block."

"But it didn't," put in Jaros.

"No, it didn't, and we also failed to track down the culprits because they didn't conduct any further espionage until the time came to retrieve Kayla. Then they tricked Jaros into going down in place of the trained agent. Jaros wasn't supposed to come back alive, but with Kayla's help he did."

"You still didn't know Ranic was behind it all?" asked Silas.

"We suspected it, but we had to be sure and we had to get any other traitors as well. That's why we let them take over Alceron; so they would all reveal themselves."

Kayla was looking worried. "Are we human?"

"Pretty much. I just cut and pasted sections of DNA to get the right results. I did generate a few small parts from scratch, but nothing major. You could just as easily have been an accident of nature."

Andrade added, "If we'd had time enough to wait for an accident."

Calron peered at Kayla strangely for a moment. "If you are worried about the twins, then don't be. I expect they will both be perfectly healthy."

Kayla's mouth fell open, but before she could say anything Breckin started dancing around the room, hugging everyone. "I'm going to be a grandpa!"

Everyone stared at Kayla, and then, when they realized what Breckin was saying, they all stared at him. Breckin was looking dotingly towards Kayla and Kayla kept switching between Calron, Breckin, and her own stomach.

Jaros complained, "Why didn't you tell me?"

Kayla shrugged her shoulders, saying, "I didn't know. Are you sure, Calron?"

Calron walked over and stared intently at Kayla's midriff for a few seconds before announcing: "About six weeks. Do you want to know the sexes?"

"No, not just yet." She looked towards Breckin. "You're my father?"

"More or less."

"Huh?"

Calron explained, "Your DNA came from about twenty sources, but a good thirty percent came from Breckin, so he's the nearest thing to a parent you've got."

"What about me?" asked Jaros.

"In your case Andrade donated about sixty percent."

"Which explains your good looks," grinned Andrade.

Breckin said, "Okay, Calron, you've told everyone else's secrets. What have you been working on so feverishly for the last few weeks?"

Calron extended his body to its full height and waited until everyone was listening intently. "What I am about to reveal to you is a triumph of science and engineering. It combines the latest advances in miniaturization, precognitive intuition, adaptive biofeedback, and biochemical synthesis."

He reached up with his arm, paused for a few moments, and then whipped the drape away. Looking around the room, Calron was startled by the complete lack of awe in the human faces looking back at him. He waited the endless fractions of a second it often took humans to react, but still nothing!

"What is it?" asked Rastus.

Ah, thought Calron, they need a demonstration to understand. "Who would like to be first? You just place your hand here," he said, indicating a sensor area on the side of the device.

Rastus reluctantly moved forwards, more as a result of a subtle nudge than because of any wish to participate. "It won't hurt?"

"No, not in the least."

Rastus placed his hand on the indicated panel and waited expectantly. After a few moments the machine began to hum, then a misty distortion appeared just above its top surface. The mist began to coalesce until it was no longer transparent. The hum subsided and the mist slowly wafted away, leaving a small purplish lump.

The room was silent. They all stared at the purple lump but nothing else happened.

"Go on," said Calron.

"Go on and what?" asked Rastus.

"Eat it."

"Eat it?"

"Yes. Isn't that what you normally do with food?"

Rastus eyed the odd-looking lump suspiciously, edging away from it.

"Are you trying to tell us," began Jaros, "that while we were fighting for our lives, you were building an auto chef?"

Before Calron could reply Kayla stepped forward and broke off a tiny piece of the odd looking substance.

"You really should let Rastus taste that one, as it was generated from his bio scan," warned Calron.

Ignoring the warning, Kayla put the piece in her mouth. While they watched her, a strange look came over her face. She said, "I knew it!" and threw her arms around Calron. "It's you, isn't it, Alfred?"

Calron was not accustomed to being hugged. While trying to maintain a degree of dignity he admitted, "I am partly he. It was necessary to split into two functional units in order that someone who couldn't be mentally detected would be able to keep an eye on you. It also gave us some insurance against Earth or Alceron being unexpectedly destroyed. And after you brought my other half with you I was able to merge back into one unit."

"I knew it," said Kayla happily, and hugged him tighter.

"You're blocking my ventilation ducts," complained Calron.

"Oh. Sorry."

"That's all right. You've always been a little overly emotional."

Rastus asked, "What did it taste like?"

Kayla searched for the appropriate word, "Scrumptious!"

Calron beamed delightedly. "Would anyone else like to try it?"

The others came forward and broke off small pieces. Each person looked thoughtful for a moment before announcing that they, too, liked it.

Later that evening, Jaros dragged Kayla out of the room and whispered, "Threatening to disown anyone who let on what it really tasted like was a little cruel; we can't keep eating the gunk indefinitely. Sooner or later someone's going to have to tell him."

"No, we won't. Mark and I lived with his cooking for years and it didn't kill us. Anyway, he'll probably get interested in something else in a day or two. Then we can go back to real food."

"That's a bit sneaky, isn't it?"

"Yes. I learned from an expert," said Kayla, and then continued in her most seductive voice: "Was that the only reason you dragged me out here?"

"No, there was one other small matter. It seems to me that it's about time I made an honest woman of you."

Kayla smiled. "Oh, it does, does it? And what if I don't want to be made into an honest woman?"

"Who cares what you want? I'm a very important person you know; a prince, no less! So stop your stalling and out with an answer. Are you going to stick by your promise of matrimony, or will I have to beat you?"

"Oh! Yes, your princeliness," said Kayla breathlessly.

"Which do you mean? Yes, I'll have to beat you; or, yes, you'll marry me?"

Kayla grinned back. "I haven't decided."

Several hours later, in the early hours of the morning, Alex kissed Nessa good night and stumbled out down the hall towards his sleeping quarters. As he reached the door an odd thought popped into his head and then, in amazement, he said, "Cripes, the butler did do it!"

THE END

www.ingramcontent.com/pod-product-compliance
Lightning Source LLC
Chambersburg PA
CBHW031330170626
46807CB00002B/637